Stream

Special Investigator

George R. Mead

E-Cat Worlds Press

This is a work of fiction. All the characters and events portrayed are creations of the imagination, nothing more, nothing less.
Comments and questions? –> gmead01@gmail.com

Stream. Special Investigator.

LCCN 2014919056

Mead, George R.
Stream. Special Investigator. /
George R. Mead.
p. cm. – Stream. Special Investigator
ISBN-13 978-0-9890927-7-7
1. Fantasy. I. Title. II. Series.

E-Cat Worlds established its publishing program as a reaction to the large commercial publishing houses currently dominating the book industry and the smaller intellectual clones. It is interested in publishing works of fiction and non-fiction that are often deemed insufficiently profitable or commercial or that are not necessarily reflective of current literary trends and fads.

E-Cat Worlds, 57744 Foothill Road, La Grande OR 97850
www.ecatworldspress.com
SAN 255-6383

In the middle of nowhere - Creativity.

First Edition:
Printed in the United States of America

Once upon a time, which is as good a way to start as any, there was a young girl named Stream.

From a very early age it was apparent that she had a grand imagination, a great curiosity, and an astonishing intellect, three attributes that her parents, Thomas and Nerza Sidling, recognized early.

Her parents would never tell her how she came to have the name she had, not why, not whatever.

But they read to her, they played with her, they did all those things that parents can do to make her a child that felt wanted, loved, protected, and nourished.

When their daughter entered the educational system they continued to work with her and they taught her how to behave in a way to be, more or less, like everyone else. They carefully explained that with her "gifts" it was a necessary thing to do as children, and adults, frequently couldn't, or weren't willing, to acknowledge or to accept someone like her.

She grew up, graduated from high school, then a series of colleges, and found a well paying job, one in which she could be what she was, a very gifted person hiding in plain sight.

Growing up in the northwest portion of the United States in a smallish, rather rural setting, Stream had developed a sense of freedom that the outdoors offered and became quite adept at back-packing and hiking into areas where few folk ever ventured.

And that is where the real tale begins.

Through The Looking Glass, So To Speak.

She was driving along a dirt road, one of the poorly maintained dirt roads in this rather empty, in terms of roads, piece of New Mexico.

She was driving rather slowly, knowing that there would be no traffic piling up behind her, and that it would easier on her truck if she didn't batter it to death by driving too fast.

The CD in her radio system was playing through its speakers, one of Nakai's flute albums. It seemed to her to be appropriate.

As she rattled along and across the ruts and bumps, she noticed, now and then, the tire tracks leaving the road and headed out into open space to somewhere unseen from the road.

At the correct spot she would do the same thing.

She was taking time off, a vacation. It was time away from work, time away from the workforce, time away from the sometimes enforced social activity, time away from the sorta urban setting that mostly surrounded her.

Taking time off was a requirement for her, a time for her mind to relax, a time to be surrounded by the quiet, the real quiet.

Finally she was there, at the correct spot. She turned off the road onto the rarely used parallel ruts that were old tire tracks.

She arrived, parked in the usual place, the one she always used when coming here. Other than the twin ruts nothing was visible from that dirt road.

She unloaded her gear, set it on the ground next to her rig, inhaled a deep breath of clear desert air, and began to organize whatever required organizing.

She was one of those folk that followed ultra-lite backpacking. Everything she was using had been carefully selected for maximum utility and minimum weight. Other than the necessary amount of water, there was as little weight as possible, food included.

Shrugging on her pack, she set out, walking in the faint game trail that headed exactly toward where she was going. She inhaled and tasted the odors of the sparse vegetation drifting past her. She turned and listened to the various small birds darting about, making their small bird calls, darting from clump to clump of brush.

For her, this was an easy hike, one she had made a number of times before. She strode along with an easy hiker's stride, slowly, slowly, sinking below the surrounding surface until she stood on the bottom of a very narrow, high-walled canyon, or draw, or crack, however one might wish to label it. The colors blended from soft rust brown to slight tans where the water had washed down from above dragging along other colors.

She had checked and rechecked the weather forecasts for this area, using a number of different sources. No rain was forecast stretching well past the time she would spend here. There were numbers of cracks and crevices that would allow water to pour down into this canyon. Not something to look forward to if one was down here.

Hitching her pack up just a tad, just a little, she strolled down the slight grade, headed for her camping spot, one, that as far as she could tell, had never been visited since ever so long ago.

It would take several hours before she got there.

So, she strolled along, watching the play of light on the high walls, listening to various sounds, coming from here and there, and relaxed, really, really relaxed.

Which, after all, was the reason for being here.

It was about two hours later when she finally arrived.

She stopped and carefully checked the immediate area, and satisfied that no-one had been, or was , around, she strolled further down the canyon and turned to face one the vertical canyon walls where water seeped from the thin crack and into a carved stone bowl. Refilling her water bottle, she turned and walked back and around the sharp bend in the canyon.

Standing in front of the pock-marked stone face she looked up and studied it. Then she began to climb, carefully placing her hands and feet into the correct spots among the many indentations.

It was a very careful ascent, one that she had worked out over many days of frustration after she had the realization what it was that she saw. That realization had come from her intensive reading in the archaeological literature of this area, and a recognition, one that she had gained from much trail and error, and hard work, of the correct path up to her, and the ancient dwellers of this place, living spot, her camping spot.

At the top of her climb, she slithered over the lip of the great cavern and stood. She walked around checking for footprints. In the back area, protected from the weather outside, the only footprints were those she had left from past trips. Back here there was always a faint dust dry smell.

Satisfied that these abandoned dwellings had not been disturbed, she set her pack against a house wall and made her camp. From this spot, across the open space to the far wall, she could see the great panel of petroglyphs made in the far distant past by those who had lived here. Strange figures, designs, and animals, the meanings of which were unknown but written about by researchers throughout the United States who often "explained" them by mainly utilizing their imaginations.

This was a good spot to camp.

Even if the weather, in spite of the several forecasts, should suddenly shift and the canyon ran wet, she would be dry. This cavern was high above the high water marks. If the wind blew down or over the high canyon walls, the depth of the cavern and the structure it held tended to buffer such storms and kept the rear area dry. And if she had to, she could follow the route that original dwellers had used to get to the upper surface, where wet would not be such a hazard to the health. It would be another very careful climb.

She sat and leaned back against the wall and began to write in her journal, a very small journal of just enough pages to last for the time she would spend here.

Finally, done for the day, she made and ate dinner, sat on the lip of the cavern, legs dangling down, and watched darkness begin to flood the canyon. Looking up, she could see the brightest stars beginning to show in the ever darkening sky.

She hitched back, stood, arranged her sleeping gear into the correct shape, stretched out and fell asleep.

Her eyes popped open.

It was dark.

Almost.

There was a thin sliver of light on the outer edge of the cavern. The moon was high enough to pour illumination into the canyon and touch that spot and wash soft light over everything in the front third of the great open space.

Then she realized that the moon wasn't the only light source.

Some of the petroglyphs were glowing, a very

soft yellow glow.

Strange, she thought. That had never happened before. In the morning she would check them and try to figure out how they did that.

Then she jerked, sat up, and slid until her back and shoulders bumped into the stone house wall.

Two of those glowing petroglyphs seemed to float free of the wall and drift toward her. They grew larger and larger as they approached.

As far as she knew there were no gasses seeping from the cavern walls that might explain what she was seeing. So why was she hallucinating like this? It hadn't happened before.

The two figures now stood at the foot of her sleeping bag and seemed to be staring at her although these glyphs had not been drawn with eyes.

A soft mist oozed from them and wrapped around until only a tall column of shimmering grey stood there.

The fog faded away and they stood there. Two human appearing individuals, apparently human, dressed in strange garb.

The one wore a dark mask helmet with yellow, round painted eyes with great dark pupils. The hair style on the mask suggested that she was female. She wore a dark blue skirt with a great cape like garment over her shoulders that hung below her knees. She held a round gourd on a stick in her right hand and a strung bow in her left.

The other figure was obviously male, bare to the waist. He, like the woman, held the same sort of gourd device in his right hand and a strung bow in his left. On his head he wore a very stylized dog-like mask that covered his entire head.

The pair stood perfectly still, and watched her.

Each shook their gourd rattles. And stopped.

"I am," said a deep female voice, a deep elder female voice, "called He'e'e in my people's tongue, a female warrior. In the very long ago I defended my people."

She shook her rattle again, and stopped.

"You are now my warrior, Stream, The Warrior. We," she gestured at her companion, "have seen this. And it is so!"

She held up the hand clenching the rattle to stop the questions she could see forming on Stream's face.

"Daughter, you, with your abilities, have been called!"

She waggled her hand toward the opening of the cavern.

"Out there is a dark thing! It is not a thing for us! It is a thing for you to get rid of!"

She looked at the other, who nodded.

"I am," rasped a male voice, "called Poko in my people's tongue. The first domestic dog was my doing. Before they were dogs they were wolves. As the dog serves my people by being his friend, so the wolves-in-spirit will serve you as your's."

He shook his rattle, and stopped.

"Daughter have no fear!" The rattle holding hand waggled toward the canyon.

"Out there is a dark thing! It is not a thing for us! It is a thing for you to get rid of!"

"Now sleep," said the pair in unison. "Enjoy the peace and quiet of this place. It is a special place for us, it is a special place for you."

The pair faded away and the only light that she could see was the narrow sliver of moon light at the edge of the cavern.

Stream slipped down and back into her sleeping bag and lay on her back staring up into the darkness where the cavern roof was, wondering if what she had just experienced was real, or just her imagination hard at work for some reason.

And fell asleep.

When she woke, it was a bright sunny day.

She yawned, stretched, and slipped from her sleeping bag. Then she wandered around the cavern searching once again for new footprints. And not finding any.

During the rest of the week, she puzzled over her strange dream, having carefully checked the large patch of petroglyphs. She made the crawl up to the surface, wandered around, and found nothing.

Finally she gave it up and merely enjoyed the rest of her vacation.

On the last day, she carefully packed everything, leaving not a trace behind, and carefully climbed down to the canyon floor, inspected it for unusual signs, found none, and headed back to where she had parked her rig.

After making the long drive on the ill-maintained and rutted road, trailing a large cloud of dust, she reached the main highway and headed for the closest large town and a book store.

Once there, she bought several illustrated books on Kachinas and stuffed them into her gear. She planned to study these once she was back in her office.

Surprise!

A week had past before she had worked her way through the pile that had accumulated in her In Box. The stack of books dealing with Kachinas still sat on top of one of the short book shelves waiting for her perusal.

Strream was dressed in her usual work clothes, loose jeans varying from blue jeans to, at times, a bright red pair, baggy cowboy shirt, usually denim, comfortable and well worn flat-heeled cowboy boots.

In the midst of finishing one of the larger problems from her In Box, her phone murmured softly. She picked it up.

"What! Boss?"

She tucked the hand set between her shoulder and ear and began to sign the pages of her sign off sheets for the several reports, grunting now and then just so he knew she was still listening.

Finished with her paper work and her phone call, she hung up the phone, rocked back in her plush swivel chair, took a sip from her large coffee cup, and watched the clear glass door of her office. At the moment there wasn't anything to see except the other side of the corridor, the empty corridor.

Her office was large with lots of room for books, shelves stuffed full. To one side sat a large workspace with computers, printers, and other electronic devices. This room pretty much contained everything that she required to do her job when she was in the office. She had another smaller side room with a bed and shower where she could sleep and refresh herself if she was deep inside some project and worked extremely late. This week she had done just that.

She watched the tall man walk up and stare at the writing on the outside of her door, *Special Investigations,* hesitate, then rap gently on the glass.

She beckoned him in, pointed at one of the comfortable chairs, and raised her eyebrows. This guy, she thought, looked like Mr. Everyone. He was so everyone she knew that no-one would ever remember him being anywhere. His clothes fit his looks. They were just everyday clothes that anyone might wear, all soft browns in color.

"Miss Stream?"

She nodded. He sat upright, but relaxed.

She waited.

He cleared his throat. And tried a tentative smile.

She waited.

"Did. Ummm, Mr. Ranpan, tell you that I was coming?"

She nodded. And waited. Watching him carefully.

"I, ahh, am, eh, your Research Assistant."

"I do not require one."

He nodded. "He, ahh, said you would say that."

She nodded back. And waited.

He sighed. "He told me that when you said that to tell you that it was not a option." He jerked to his feet.

"I do not want to be someone who is in between you two while you engage in some sort of bureaucratic warfare. But I am qualified."

He jerked a rather crumpled roll of papers from the side pocket on this casual jacket, tossed it on her desk, and spun toward the door.

"SIT!"

He turned back, eyes wide at her tone of voice. "What?"

She pointed at the same chair. "Right there."

Then she picked up the papers, smoothed them on the edge of her desk, and began to read them.

He sat and stared as she rapidly flipped them over, one by one. Flip, flip, flip, flip . . .

"O.K.," she said, looking up from the last page. "You are on probation. Starting now. And just call me Stream, it is my first name."

Her eyes wandered over his clothes. "No tie?" She sat back and suppressed her smile. He had actually blushed.

Hastily reaching into his jacket pocket, he yanked out a rather crumpled, balled up tie, and shook it out.

"Stop!"

He jerked.

"We don't have a dress code here. It was a joke. Sorta. Put that thing away."

He stuffed it back into his side pocket.

She yanked over a thick folder that had been sitting on one corner of her desk.

"You may start with this." She pointed. "That desk over there. Use whatever you wish, need, or require. I want to know what you think about it."

She stood. "I will be back in twenty minutes. What do I call you?"

"Lou."

She nodded and left him to his chore. We'll see, she thought, how qualified you really are.

Stream returned in exactly twenty minutes.

He was sitting at the desk doing something on the computer. The thick folder sat to one side with a thick note pad on top. She could see that it was covered with writing.

She sat at her desk.

"What do your initials stand for and tell me about your last name."

He turned off the computer and spun around in the swivel chair.

"Lucien Prince Woulfe, the family name came to Ireland with the Normans in the twelfth century. My ancestors fled during the potato famine. I really do prefer Lou."

"So, what did you think of that report? Lou?"

Without looking, he reached sideways and picked up the note pad, nodded at her, then looked at the top page, and cleared his throat.

"Page one, paragraph one, third sentence states that . . . "

She sat still as still as he began to take her through the report, page by page.

Well, she thought, he is certainly as good as he said he was in those materials he had dropped on her desk. He had understated his abilities, if anything.

Her eyes flicked to the clock on the wall behind him, held up her hand, palm out, and stopped him. Twenty minutes had gone by and he was a long way from finished.

"Fine. You'll do. You're hired."

He nodded, one quick nod, reached sideways and dropped the note pad back on top of the thick folder.

"The person that wrote that is no longer employed by us, by me."

She received another quick nod.

She stood. He lurched to his feet.

"Well, let's go see what The Boss has for us, shall we?"

She led him down the long corridor, around the corner, and into the correct room.

Well, This Is A Fine Howdy-Do!

They piled into Stream's truck, a weathered brown color. She drove toward the edge of town, toward the oldest edge of town.

This area had numbers of old, some said ancient, adobe homes, most with high walls, some capped with light red or brown curved roofing tiles, that surrounded the property. The street-side walls sat right at the edge of the poorly maintained street with heavy wooden gates the opened onto the interior parking spot.

At one of these, Stream parked, nose of the truck almost touching the gate, jumped out, shoved the gate wide, jumped back in, and drove inside, and parked, switched off the ignition.

"Come on in, I need to get my gear."

She jumped down and headed for the front door, heavy wood with a small window near the top, lifted the latch and strode inside, Lou trailing behind her, his curiosity at a high level, eyes checking the yard, then the inside of the large room they stepped into.

Two steps in, she jolted to a halt.

"Who are you?" she demanded. "And what are you doing in my house?"

Lou stepped to one side and one step behind

Stream, ready to eject unwanted visitors.

A man and a woman smiled at her. They were standing in the middle of the large room. They were both young, about Stream's age.

"I am Lupe," stated the woman. "This is my brother, Luis."

The pair were taller than Stream, but shorter than Lou, dark skinned, dark eyes, dark hair. Both had a rather compact build although the brother was much wider than his sister.

"Grandmother Garcia sent us two days ago to collect your mail, and to check the house and the garden," explained Lupe. "Grandfather was feeling poorly, so she sent us."

She stepped close to Stream. "She knew that you hadn't been here for a few days and knew that you often remained at your place of work." She frowned.

"We walked from her house late in the evening. As we came near we saw two figures run from the gate and down the street." She pointed the direction that they had run, then waggled that hand.

"Given the lack of street lights in this part of town, we saw no details nor did we decide to chase after them, so we came inside, after closing the outside gate." Her frown darkened.

"As far as we could tell, nothing was taken, however it appears, from the mess, that they searched your office and study." She sighed.

"We tidied up, a little, but thought that it would

be best to not do much as you should be able to tell whether they actually took anything or not. Perhaps we interrupted them before they could." She shrugged.

"Grandmother told us to stay here until you returned."

Stream nodded at them.

"Stay here, Lou. Have some coffee, I can smell it."

She strode toward one end of the house to check on things.

Lupe directed him toward the kitchen, a well furnished and equipped kitchen.

"This way."

As Lou, seated at the kitchen table with Lupe and Luis, was working on his second cup of coffee and pastry, Stream walked in, filled a cup, took a pastry and a bite from it, and joined them at the table.

"Obviously they were searching for something but nothing was taken. Whatever they thought to find, they didn't find it." She laughed.

"There is nothing work related here. It is all kept in a secure area in my office." She shrugged. And smiled at the pair. "So whatever it was that they thought to find, they were out of luck. Not much in here worth stealing."

"Tell your Grandmother thanks for me. I'll talk with her in a few days. I'll take care of cleaning up in here."

The pair nodded to her, stood, and left.

She look over her coffee cup at Lou.

"Do you have back-packing gear? We are going to be in some fairly lonesome country for 2 or 3 days, or so."

"Yep."

"Good! We'll go by your place after I get my things reorganized. Be right back."

She hurried back to her truck, grabbed her gear from the back, and headed for the room where she stored all her gear.

She had put off doing this when she had returned and so now she had to do this little chore.

It didn't take long and soon they were on their way to Lou's place. He gave her directions.

Desolation?

After rattling along and over a number of marginal roads, wheel ruts and barely visible indications of past travel, Stream parked, on a bare spot, turned off her rig, jumped out, pocketed her keys, and began to unload their gear from the back.

As soon as both of them had settled their backpacks on their backs, she pointed at the white rig tucked between two very large rocks, a very big, four-door sedan.

"The guy that we are interested in owns that. We tracked it to this spot a few days ago."

Her arm swivelled.

"There is a trail right there, that slight notch, believe it or not. So we are going to take a hike and see whether we can pick up his tracks and follow them to him. As far as we know he is not much of an outdoors type of person and this is not a good place for someone like that to be wandering around in. So, we should be able to catch up with him."

She led Lou over to the parked vehicle and tugged the driver's door open.

After making a search, she crawled back out, and

circled around the vehicle slowly, stopped and peered underneath, and then wandered back to where he stood watching her.

"At least he didn't bother to lock it. Wonder why. Of course there might not be anyone that would come this way for months and months."

She pointed. "Narrow heels, smooth soles. I'd guess cowboy boots. Not exactly the sort of thing to take a long hike in. He might not go too far then. We can only hope."

She started off.

"Nice day for a walk. Wonder how far he got before he camped."

The sun rose higher and began to glare down on them and everything else.

The trail pitched over the edge through the slight notch and began to wander along the side slope until it reached the bottom of the wide and dry arroyo.

Everything in sight was a light yellow mixed with soft rust brown and all shades in between. A few bushes grew here and there, mostly dead and water worn.

"Desolate spot."

She laughed.

"What?"

"All in the eye of the beholder. After awhile you will begin to see more that the rock and the dirt."

When they reached the bottom they could see the traces of faint and smudged footprints overlain by animal tracks as the trail headed upstream, upstream that is if there had been water flowing down here. The animal tracks had come and gone in both directions.

They headed in the direction the boot tracks went.

Lou pointed.

"Does whoever that is know where they are going?"

Stream wobbled her head.

"There are a few long ago abandoned cabins, of a sort, up this way, abandoned ruins, a couple of poor attempts at mining. That stuff reflects the history of this area."

"Seems like a strange place to hide. He would have done better to head into a high density population area."

"Yep." She nodded. "Perhaps we can ask him when we get there."

Slowly, ever so slowly, as they hiked along, the side walls began to rise and the width of the arroyo narrowed.

Stream pointed up at one bench.

"First stop."

Lou looked. He could just see a bit of grey weathered wooden something up there.

While they had been hiking, she had checked his clothes and his gear. None of it was brand new, just off the shelf, so she figured that he had spent some time in the outdoors. He did have a slightly weathered look as well. She decided that this didn't really detract from his appearance at all.

When they reached the top, Lou took a quick scan of the area.

Stream led him up the correct trail and shook her head. "Probably not. But we will check every place."

Once they had walked to the top they could see that the structure was standing, more or less. It appeared as if the only reason that it had not collapsed into a mass of twisted timber appeared to be the very large boulder that it had slumped against. She led him around and to the only doorway. The door had fallen outward and lay in front of the structure. Lou peered through the remains of the only window, it had fallen inside, and could see that no one was at home.

"Long time since anyone was here."

"Yep. We will just walk along up here for a bit." She pointed. "You can see that next structure from here."

Lou started in the direction indicated, squinted, his eyes scanning back and forth.

"Ahhh," he said. "It looks to be in worse shape that this place, from what I can tell."

"Yep." She strolled off. "No hurry."

When they arrived at the collapsed structure they found that only the portion of one corner was still intact. It made a rather small cave like space amidst the jumbled weathered wood building remains.

Stream shrugged off her backpack, retrieved her

flashlight, knelt, and shined it inside the dark space.

"Rodent nest, otherwise empty."

She stood, replaced her flashlight, and swung her pack into place.

"The next stop is an old mining attempt. It is on the other bench."

Lou followed her as she strolled along near the edge of the arroyo.

"Did you see those tiny flowers back there?" he asked.

She laughed. "Told you!"

Finally she clambered down the side and led him up the other side of the now very narrow arroyo. As they reached the top, Lou cleared his throat, loudly.

"What?"

"Well, ah um, I was wondering who it is that we are searching for, or to find, or whatever."

Stream grinned at him, "So O.K. I'll tell you. But no laughing."

He stared at her. "Umm?"

She winked.

"His name is Frederick Furguson, known far and wide among certain sectors of the population as Fergy, or in some cases as Ferg."

Lou smiled but sucked in the laugh.

She nodded.

"Fergy is known as a money handler, that is, someone who knows how to see that it comes from over there and that it gets to somewhere else safely. He is, or perhaps was, very, very good at doing that. For Fergy it was a very good money making process. Lots and lots of money. He called it a business. Fergy had a rare talent for things like that and certain folk paid generously for him to do just that."

"Uh huh. But?"

"But!" She smiled at him. And explained.

"But there is always a squirrel in the cage. This particular squirrel felt that Fergy shouldn't be a free lance artist sorta guy but ought to work for him as an employee."

"Ah."

"Worse."

"Worse?"

"Yep. Fergy, now part of the group, would get, let's say, a rather reduced salary, with the excess going into someone's coffer other than his."

"Ah, indeed. And . . . so?"

"Not long ago, Fergy snuggled up to my boss at one of the better restaurants. And slipped a rather stuffed briefcase to him. Shortly thereafter, Fergy disappeared."

"Um."

"And here we are."

"Eh."

"Missing person hunt, so to speak."

"How about we stop for a snack?"

She pointed.

"There?"

"There."

When they finally arrived at "there" Lou could see that the arroyo had bent sharply to the right, narrowed, and then broadened out again.

"The rock right there is a narrow dike of hard stuff," explained Stream. He headed them up to the top.

She walked over and sat. "Pull up a boulder, we can snack for a bit." She smiled at him as he did. Sit on one of the right-sized boulders for sitting upon.

As she opened something and took a bite, she mumbled around the crumbs, "Welcome to The Little Wonder Mine." She indicated the framing around the dark opening. "They went back a couple of hundred feet or so. Their ore cart is parked back there on the rails."

Lou looked around. One tiny, weather beaten but still somehow standing shack with a stove pipe still sticking up through the roof. The framing around the tunnel opening were large, rough cut timbers. He could see more of the same disappearing into the gloom of the tunnel. The narrow gauge rail ran to the edge of the arroyo apparently to dump debris over the edge. Looking down he could see that heavy runoff, or flash floods, had carried it away.

"Pretty quiet out here."

"Yep," she agreed. "Wait here, be right back."

She took her flashlight and headed into the darkness. "Just checking for footprints."

In a moment she strode back outside.

"No visitors of the human kind."

She checked the shed, came back, and picked up her pack, flashlight once again properly stowed.

"Ready?"

"Sure." He stood. Yanked his pack up and into place, and looked for any sign of structures upstream, and shrugged.

"Spick and span."

"Some distance from here you'll see the ruins, dwellings of the long ago folk. Not a bad place to camp if you are prepared.

They dropped down into the arroyo and trudged onward.

Lou thought the grade seemed to be getting, ever so gently, steeper. He looked at the side walls and noted the scoring way above their heads. The water must really roar down through here when it rains higher up. He checked the piece of sky that he could see ahead of them. It was a clear blue, not a cloud to be seen. From here.

"I always check the weather forecasts first," she said, noticing the direction he was staring.

It turned out, for Lou, to be quite a long walk to the ruins. This gave him lots of time to examine his environment, and, ever so carefully, his boss.

She, he decided, was a very relaxed person in her own unique way. She was obviously athletic, the way she moved told him that. She carefully kept herself unknown but as she talked about this or that he got a peek, now and then, of the real person behind the carefully controlled mask, the person kept ever so carefully out of sight. There was so much more to her than he suspected anyone really knew.

As they rounded another of the bends in what was becoming a rather twisting arroyo, she pointed.

"Up there. We have to follow that game trail and then you will see them."

She started up the game trail as it worked its way to the top.

As they crested the top, she laughed, pointing at a trail of faint but visible footprints.

"Well, well, and well, well. I do believe Fergy is up here, somewhere."

They stopped, giving Lou a chance to look over the series of stacked stone structures.

"Quiet a complex." He walked toward a corridor that appeared to lead into the center of the cluster.

"Hold up! I found Fergy's trail. His footprints go over this way." She pointed. "It looks like he headed for that one toward this corner."

Lou hurried over and followed her around one of the structures and watched as she ducked through the low doorway.

"MERDE!"

He ran in after her.

Fergy sat wedged in a far corner, chin resting on his chest. He looked dusty.

Stream knelt next to the body and carefully

searched each pocket. Then she stood.

"Can't tell what he took, but it did the job. He didn't leave a note. And he obviously didn't shoot himself. The forensic crowd will have find whatever there is to find. The medicos will figure out the rest." She sighed.

Then she stepped outside and waited for him to join her.

"We can camp over there. After we get back to the rig I will radio in and they can send in a chopper and do what needs doing, including bring Fergy out for burial." She sighed again.

"Can't leave him here although he probably thought that was now it was going to work out."

She led him past several of the buildings and stopped next to a mostly complete structure.

"We can camp here and stroll out in the morning."

She shrugged off her pack and began to take out what was needed.

"Tomorrow, we'll go to my place, then your's. The day after that we'll do a thorough search of Fergy's place."

She sat on the spread out sleeping bag and pad and leaned back against the handy wall.

"Nice view from here. Think?"

Lou smiled as he spread out his stuff.

"Yes. It is."

He jerked his thumb over his shoulder.

"Fergy was here for awhile."

She nodded.

"Figured that we had no need to hurry after him. Camping out here, he wasn't going to go anywhere. Big surprise."

Lou nodded.

Pretty Strange All Right

Stream and Lou walked back to where they had parked. Once there, she contacted headquarters, reported what they had found, And were assured that forensics and medical teams would be there as soon as possible and that she and her assistant need not remain.

"Nice day for a walk," Lou had observed as they had strolled back.

"Certainly is."

As they stashed their gear in the back of her truck she pointed at the other vehicle. "They'll come and take it away and then go over it looking for anything that they can find."

They piled into her rig and headed out.

After following the wheel ruts, a rather vague dirt road, a poorly maintained dirt road, a badly patched paved road, they headed for town on the paved two-lane county road.

"Hungry?"

Lou nodded. "Getting there."

"Spicy food all right?"

"Sure."

She winked at him.

"Then you are invited to dinner. I bought a new Tex-Mex cookbook and want to try out a couple of the recipes."

"Ummm."

"What?"

"Is this proper?"

"Eating spicy food?"

"Us having dinner at your place. You are my boss."

"So?"

He frowned.

"Sexual harassment and boss-employee relationships and things like that there."

Stream laughed.

"Huh?"

"Two adults, one male, one female, have been camping together, not chaperoned. What's the difference?"

"Umm."

"It is just dinner and then we go back to work."

"Oh. We do?"

"Heh, heh. We are going to Fergy's place and search it from top to bottom, assuming that no-one else has already done that. We'll see when we get there. Could be a very long night so eat lots."

"O.K."

"Of course." She sighed.

"What?"

"Am I going to have trouble with you?"

Lou laughed, a soft gentle laugh.

"No."

"Good."

She swung around the correct corner and slowed up. The truck headlights had reflected from the rear bumper of a vehicle parked in front of her place.

"Now what?"

It was a police car. The gate was wide open and lots of bright light shown past the front of the car and across the street.

She parked right behind the police car and jumped out.

A large uniform stepped from the car.

"Stream?"

"Big John." She waggled her hand. "My new assistant, Lou."

Big John shook Lou's hand, enveloping it in his.

Lou could see where his nickname came from. He was a very large person.

"What's up, B.G.?"

"You own a dog or two?"

"Nope. With my work schedule and all it wouldn't work out. Why?"

"Let's go inside."

He led them through the gate and pointed at police tape surrounding the center of her parking space and large stain inside it.

"We received a complaint, a phoned in complaint. One of your neighbors heard screaming and yelling from inside your place. They though we ought to check."

B.G. scuffed the edge of one boot on the gravel.

"It was dark in here when we arrived. No light on anywhere. I flashed my light around, the front door was wide open and they were laying right there." He pointed.

"Two very dead bodies, right there. Both young, un, youngish males. They looked like they had been mauled by dogs, large dogs."

She stared at him, brows furrowing.

"Dogs? Was my gate closed?"

"Uh huh."

"No way dogs could have gotten inside then."

B.G. shrugged.

"What it looked like to me. The coroner will see whatever. Then we'll know for sure. Already sent their prints in, see if they pop." He shrugged one massive shoulder. "Probably will."

Then he started for the front door.

"None of us went in. Yet. Wanted to wait until you came home so you could see if anything was in the process of being taken."

He stopped her with one wide swung arm.

"It is a little messy in there. You can see the blood trail heading out the door toward the parking area. I just peeked in. Waiting for some of our troop to arrive. Do the usual thing." He looked at her. "You've been keeping them busy today, ah, tonight."

She nodded.

"We haven't had dinner yet, B.G. Can we do that and return, hopefully after you are done?"

"Sure." He looked at his watch. "How about a leisurely dinner for a couple of hours. That ought to do it, I hope. Your boss has some folk coming as well."

She smiled at him and spun around.

"Let's go Lou, I'm hungry."

As they walked back to her truck, she mumbled, "It is going to be a longer night than I thought."

She drove down two blocks, hooked a left turn, and parked in the middle of the block. There weren't any street lights in this area either.

Lou could see cars and trucks parked haphazardly on either side of the street in the dim light that shown from a sizable, but not very well washed window.

Stream jumped from the truck.

"Rotten decor, peculiar service, really good food, if you like Mexican chow minus all that sour cream and stuff."

She headed across the street and threw the door wide and strode inside, Lou trailing along.

The interior was one large room with a kitchen door to one side that stood wide open. Straight ahead there was a bar lined with stools of various vintages occupied with a few folk also of various vintages.

A few small wooden tables, badly worn and stained from use, were scattered, one here, one there, in no discernable order. Along the left hand wall as they stood facing the bar were some wooden bench seats attached to that wall with small wooden, rectangular tables set in from of them. The tables were just large enough for two people to sit comfortably next to each other.

Stream pointed at one, more or less in the center of the line along the wall.

"That one! My treat. I'll order."

Lou headed for that table, she headed for the bar and talked with the bartender. Then she returned carrying two large steins fills with a dark brown beer. She had order two large platters of assorted foods.

She plunked down the steins and settled on the bench seat next to him.

"I ordered lots. We'll need it." She took a long sip from her stein.

They sat in comfortable silence, sipped, and watched the bar tender head to the kitchen after a high pitched voice yelled something.

He reentered the main room, a very large platter held in each hand. Thumping them down he hurried away and returned with a large stack of tortillas on a round plate, two bowls of salsa, one red, one green. Everything was more or less dumped on the table.

"Refried beans," stated Stream. "Enchiladas, one chicken, one pork, one beef, flour tortillas, two small tamales, properly wrapped in corn shucks, chili rellenos, red and green chili sauce. Yummy!"

One more trip and napkins, then knives, forks, and spoons clattered onto the table. He hurried back to his place behind the bar.

"It is rather unique," observed Lou softly.

"Yep." She began to dump red and green salsa here and there on the various offerings on the platter. Tearing a tortilla in half, she used one half to scoop up beans and took a bite.

When it was obvious that the pair were done with their meal, the bartender removed all the debris, returned with two more filled steins and took away the empties, and once again returned behind the bar.

"You always eat like this?" Lou nudged her shoulder with his. "Mere curiosity."

She nodded. "Sure, burn up lots of calories."

He slumped, legs straight out, and stared at the table top, obviously thinking about something.

She took a sip and watched a large rangy fellow detach himself from the bar and head for their table.

He stopped in front of their table and stared at Stream.

"Hi, purty lady."

"Hi, yourself."

"Join us!" He waggled one hand at the bar.

"Nope. I already have company."

He kicked the bottom of one of Lou's boots.

"Your boy friend won't mind, will ya, guy."

"Go away," he said.

His boot bottom got kicked again.

Lou slowly raised his head and looked up through his eyebrows at their visitor.

"Go . . . away . . . while . . . you . . . are . . . able."

His voice seemed to be coming from somewhere deep in his chest. He didn't blink.

The man's eyes flew wide at whatever he saw, or thought that he saw, hastily backed up, and headed for the outside door.

Stream stared at him as he disappeared to the outside, and wondered what had just happened.

"What did you do?"

Lou straightened up and slid from behind the table and stood. "Told him to go away. Shall we?"

Stream shrugged, slid sideways, and stood, dropped a number of bills on the table top, and headed for the door, still wondering how Lou had frightened that guy so badly.

Soon they were driving in a more well illuminated area. She set her curiosity aside for now and began to think about Fergy.

Finally on the far side of town they entered an area of large and expensive living where she slowly drove along one of the streets and finally pulled into a driveway and up to three stories of glass and artwork.

"Fergy's place," she explained as she walked around the back of the truck and began to hand Lou bundles of flat corrugated white-faced cardboard.

"Banker's boxes, so called. We'll put them together as we need."

Hauling a batch of keys from a side pocket, she soon had the front door open.

"You search the first floor, I'll do the second. Then we will work the third floor." She took one of the bundles from him. "Take anything that might tell us something. Stack a filled box near the front door. We'll load everything once we're done."

She pointed. "Fergy's place has an elevator." She walked over and jabbed a button, stepped through the door, and said as the door slowly closed, "See ya whenever."

A Different View

Ztrich sat in his modestly sized office furnished with modest furniture and looked over his modest desk at his two most senior staff and long-term friends sitting in modest chairs, comfortably slouching, facing him.

His office was located in one of the older, more modest office buildings in Portland, Oregon.

Z, as he was called throughout his organization, took a sip from his coffee cup and nodded at the others, who also held coffee cups and took a sip now and then.

In their carefully crafted organizational structure, "modest" was the watchword. How ever much money any single member of the organization gained, everything about them was to be modest. There would be no-one living with conspicuous consumption, nothing to attract attention, no $100,000 cars parked in the driveway or garage, no megamansions. All members of the organization knew this and they also knew that if they failed in this minor cultural value, then doing that would make Mr. Z. very unhappy.

The last member who had failed to pay attention had lived in a great two-story mansion with a three-car garage, a gigantic swimming pool, and a tennis court.

One night, an explosion had scattered the house, the garage, and the inhabitants of that residence, far and wide, living a crater where the basement had been. Investigators had concluded that it had been a faulty hot water heater in the basement. And that had been that. Modest living was now valued as a survival mechanism.

Z looked at his friend and nodded at him as he set his coffee cup down on the desk top.

James. L. took a sip and then set his coffee cup near the front edge of the desk top.

"Fergy killed himself. Two hikers wandering around in the boonies found his remains. The body was lying inside some old ruins. The coroner's report stated that he had taken massive overdoes of several over-the-counter products. When the body was found, Fergy had been dead for a few days."

Ralph set his coffee cup on the desk top, close at hand, cleared his throat.

"Someone ransacked Fergy's joint and cleaned house. It looks like they took everything not nailed down."

Z nodded at him.

"The cops down there haven't a clue as to who did this trick. It appears to have happened all in a single evening. Fergy's place is situated in such a manner that no nosey neighbor could see a thing."

Ralph leaned back and looked at James L.

James L. nodded.

"There is a smallish, special cop of some kind special unit, down there. She was known to be getting very curious about Fergy and his business dealings. I sent a couple to check out her house seeing as she is their primary investigator, apparently called a Special Investigator. They didn't find anything on their first visit."

He cleared his throat.

"They died on their second visit."

"Caught by this investigator?" asked Z.

"Nope. The report says that feral dogs jumped them. The investigator's house in way out on the very edge of a rather run down neighborhood that looks out at acres and acres of sage and desert. The cops and the coroner agree on cause of death."

Z sighed.

"We are looking for a replacement," stated Ralph. "But Fergy was an, ummm, unique individual. And he didn't train anyone in how he did things, at least as far as anyone knows."

Z nodded.

"Send," he said, "a couple of very careful guys to keep an eye on this special investigator for awhile. If nothing is going on, just leave. No action, just look and learn."

Z smiled. "And watch out for dogs."

The pair stood and left the room.

Z swivelled around and looked out the window.

It was a nice day. Time to take a stroll and enjoy

it. He did his best thinking while strolling along, doing nothing in particular.

Two days later, a pair of businessmen, strolled from the local airport, rented a mid-priced sedan, and drove into town. All their luggage carried the logo of some kind of business of their sides.

Well, Well, Well.

They were driving from the office to a small restaurant some distance away.

"What happened to all that stuff that we hauled away?"

It was three days since they had visited Fergy's place.

Stream waggled one hand at him.

"The techno-geeks are prowling around in Fergy's computers, he had a number of them, his cell phones, also a number of them, tablets, etc., to see what they will find. The Squirrel is working on all the paper stuff."

Lou snorted.

"Techno-geeks I understand. Squirrel?"

"A young woman who has special talents. She has Aspergers. She is very, very smart and has a rather different way of seeing things. She will go through everything in every box, squirreling around so to speak, hence the nickname. Rala sees connections that most people do not, or can see. She will remember everything and find those connections. Her talent is coupled with an intense focus on whatever she is doing. Her office has two rooms, one is the storeroom. No windows on the outside hallway so she has no distractions. In addition her rooms are heavily sound proofed. No one is allowed to just pop in to visit or to start asking questions. It interrupts her process. When she comes out for coffee, or lunch, or a snack, then and only then, may you talk with her, if she wishes. She actually likes to talk with people."

"Interesting."

"Uh huh. Many companies, organizations, could really use and benefit from folk with her talents except that they are unaware of that talent or, mostly, it is not what they learned in their business courses and thus it is unknown or not understood at all."

"Ummm."

"Yep. The usual problem."

Stream shrugged and glanced over at him.

"Look carefully in your side mirror. See that rather ordinary looking car back there?"

He did. "Uh huh."

"They are following us." She laughed.

"And we," she added, "are following them, in a manner of speaking. We know where they are staying. Think that we ought to give them a visit?"

"Nope."

"Oh?"

"Wait and see."

"What I thought. Also."

She parked her truck in front of the restaurant.

"Hope you like Thai."

"Yep."

It was a fairly upscale place, several notches of nicer that any of the places that Stream had dragged him to before.

She nodded at the head waiter, stood and talked very quietly with him for a few moments, then he escorted them over to a table set in a corner. It was one of the rather quiet and private places. The odor of curry and condiments hit their nostrils as a waiter walked by carrying someone's order.

Lou looked at the interior decor. "Nice." He pulled out her chair. "Smells good."

She smiled at him and sat.

She smiled even wider as some of the food that she had ordered began to arrive.

"I ordered spring rolls for appetizers, then shrimp with peanut sauce, chicken with chili and cabbage, egg plant with chicken, beef with fresh ginger, lots of fried rice."

After they had eaten several of the small appetizers and as soon as the main dishes arrived, she poured their tea cups full.

"Across the room, more or less in the direction you are facing, check out that alien pair, for this culture, of business types with the goofy green and yellow, logos on their briefcases leaning against their chair legs."

Lou took a sip, and munched on a small piece of

food left on his plate.

"Uh huh."

"Those are the guys that have been following us in that sorta average looking rental car. Our in-house wizards say that the logo doesn't exist for any company in the world, big or little. So, between that little piece of information and the way that they dress, it suggests that those two have no idea of local customs and culture. No business type here, or most who visit, would dress like that. Not much of a disguise."

"Well," he said, "maybe they are not trying to hide. A message that says we know who you are and that we can find you."

Stream laughed.

"What?"

"We already know who they are. Some of our sneaky types already got their fingerprints from their suite."

"Huh?"

She nudged him with an elbow.

"We have folk so invisible out there that no-one ever notices them. They pay attention to anyone that might follow one of us, anyone from work. They are known as The Shadow Crew."

Lou grinned at her. "Working here just gets more and more interesting all the time."

She nodded as their orders arrived, took a sip from her cup.

"So we just let them follow along and as long as

they behave they are safe." She began to serve them from the several platters.

"We have a lot of talented people," she added.

Stream began to eat, totally ignoring the watchers across the room.

Adventure?

"Vacation time!" announced Stream as she locked her office door and then headed them down the hall toward the outside.

"What?" Lou stared at her.

"I thought that I would go camping, a little."

Lou stopped and frowned at her back until she stopped walking and turned around.

"What?" She frowned back at him.

"I have only been working for you for what, about a month or so?"

She grinned at him.

"Wellllll," she drawled. "We have been putting in long hours, six days a week. Folk are working on the bundle that he handed to the boss. And we still have two pseudo-businessmen following us around. So, at the moment, we have no reports to write."

"And?"

"And, it is time for a little rest and relaxation. We have to stay fresh. It doesn't pay to burn out, to get overly fatigued, stuff like that there!"

"Ummmmmm. O.K." Lou nodded. And wondered. As far as he could tell, she doesn't ever seem to get tired. He was rapidly coming to the conclusion that his immediate boss must burn up thousands and thousand of calories, enough that she ought to glow in the dark. He nodded at her again.

"It is certainly a unique place to work."

She smiled. "Wanna come along, plenty of open space, plenty of quiet. Just primitive camping."

"Mind if I skip, ummmmm, this time?"

"No problemo, chico. I'll be bok, as Arnold says. In this instance in about four days."

Stream spun around and headed for the outer door, saying over her shoulder, "Need a lift?"

"Nope. Think that I will just walk, need some exercise. Ummm, have a good, ahh, trip."

She swung the door wide and waited until he passed through and indicated with her chin the sorta nondescript car parked down the street.

"If those two try to do anything you do whatever you feel like doing. O.K.?"

"Ummmmm, sure."

"O.K. See ya!"

She hurried to her truck, jumped in, and roared from the parking area.

Lou watched her head down the street, followed at a moderate distance by their two watchers.

He shrugged and strolled slowly the other way toward his lodgings.

Far, far, far out, on top of a small hill, far from

civilization, as she thought of the place where she worked, Stream set up her camp. The cooler in the back of her truck would stay cool for her planned four days. It held two blocks of ice, some containers of yogurt, and a bag of mixed greens for salad and the jar of salad dressing.

The rest of her food was either dried or in cans, cans because she wasn't backpacking this time.

So, she thought, she had all the comforts of home, in a manner of speaking.

The drive to this spot had taken the better part of the day. It was far from town, the roads, if they could be called that, were minimal and slow driving, often very slow driving.

But now, back propped up by the rear tire, she ate her supper and watched darkness creeping across the landscape. And as she ate she listened to the quiet of evening slowly settling around her.

She sighed happily at the comfort she felt being out here. It was too bad Lou hadn't come. She felt that it would have been good for him, also.

But finally, after watching the stars cluster the dark sky and the moon rise, she settled her sleeping gear into the shape she preferred and faded into sleep.

The first rays of morning sun woke her.

So she rose as well, did what needed doing, fixed breakfast, ate it, and watched a coyote wandering along far down below, apparently not bothered by her presence up here. High overhead a couple of winged predators began to glide in ever widening circles.

Then she took a short hike, just wandering along, sorta like that coyote, she thought, and returned to camp. And took a nap.

She planned to do much the same thing for the four days: eat, sleep, hike a little, nap.

At the end she would be ready for work and whatever might come her way.

It was the third night when strange woke her.

Her eyes flew open, She lay still and wondered why she was suddenly awake. She slowly, carefully twisted her head from side to side. And saw it.

She knew that there were no wolves around here, so how come she could see one right there. The shape was much to large to be a coyote. And there were no wild dogs out here either.

It sat, still as still, head lowered, watching something down the hill, down toward the open arroyo below.

Then it flowed to its feet and slipped silent shadow over the edge and out of her sight.

In the morning, she thought, in the morning I will check the tracks left behind and see what my strange visitor really was.

In the morning that is what she did. The tracks, such as they were, were mere smudges in the dust. It appeared that the evening breeze, gentle as it had been, had mostly erased them. She shrugged, whatever it had been was just going to have to remain a mystery.

So, off and on, she spent time erasing her camping traces, and hiked around searching for tracks, just to see if she could figure out from which direction her nocturnal visitor had come from. With no success. She decided trekking down the steep slope toward the arroyo was not necessary.

She pulled into her place late in the afternoon, checked what little mail was piled on her kitchen table by her house sitters/watchers and headed for the shower for a very long session of getting clean and hot water.

Samuel Anabail and Henry "Hank" Winston had been a two-man team for years. They had been sent way out here, as they saw it, to keep an eye on that special investigator, whatever that meant, who was poking around in the late Fergy's business.

It was that poking around that was making their ultimate boss a wee bit nervous. So they did their job, as they interpreted it to be. They watched and reported, every day.

Two days ago James L. had told them that she was to be eliminated, as quietly as possible.

During their on-going surveillance in town they had managed to stick tracking devices on her truck. But someone they never saw kept removing them.

Finally, in desperation, they had snuck into her house, having spent hours checking the entire area around it for unwanted observers. In this case they had been successful.

So they snuck into her house, in spite of having been ordered to never do that, and glued a very tiny thing to a piece of her camping gear.

Conveniently for them, Stream had taken that piece with her on this trip.

Now, having spent, for them, two miserable days, watching her from afar through powerful lens, they knew her routine well and decided that they would take care of "the problem" on the third night.

Late, late, late at night, Samuel remained in their observation spot while Hank, who was much better at this than Samuel, crept ever so carefully through the darkness toward their target who had been sound asleep for a long time.

Samuel watched his cohort through the best night vision equipment that could be bought or stolen.

He traced Hank as he slipped across the sandy bottom and started, ever so slowly up the slope toward their target.

The pair were not using any kind of communication equipment as they felt it was not something that would be required way out here in the boonies. After all, there were no neighbors who might look out a window at an inconvenient time for their usual activities. After all this was not a urban setting.

Suddenly Samuel gasped, and quickly muffled his surprise.

Something large, more shadow than shape, had just slipped off the top of that hill and headed down the slope. He checked Hank who was still moving a careful path upward, apparently unaware of anything coming his way.

All Samuel could do was to watch.

Hank slipped behind a large clump of brush and scraggly trees.

Samuel watched and waited. Hank did not appear.

Then Samuel saw what appeared to be a rather large dog trot up the draw between where he lay and where he had last seen Hank. It disappeared into a sage thicket.

Samuel waited, gun in hand, checking and rechecking all the area below and across from his position until the sun came up and flooded the scene before him with light. He packed his gear and watched the camp spot.

Then he saw her rise, make and eat breakfast and begin to put away her gear, wander about, and then drive away.

When she was far from sight, Samuel headed down and over toward the last place that he had last seen Hank.

He found Hank lying between the brush and the

trees, gun still holstered, flat on his back, his throat a ragged mass of red and torn flesh.

Samuel could see a large dusty paw print on Hank's shirt.

Samuel twisted away and ran as hard as he could, stopping frequently, gun in hand, pointing here and there, but there was nothing out there.

When he finally returned to their rented suite, he made a single phone call, hastily packed, checked out, and took the first plane available at the local airport.

"Okey dokey!" she announced as she bounced into her office having noticed Lou was already there and doing something on one of the computers.

"Wuzz zup?" She grinned at his startled expression.

It was the second day after she had returned from her petite piece of R'n'R.

"One of our two watch dogs," he said, "checked out about the same time you got back to town. No one has seen the other one since about that same time."

"It's a puzzlement," she stated sagely. Stream had watched the movie, *The King and I*, last night.

"Uh huh?"

"Got your hiking boots on, or handy?"

He lifted one leg and waggled a foot at her. "Yep."

"Then we're off to see a dead body. Dead about two-three days body, so I've been told. Folk want us to take a look at it before they haul it back to town."

It was late afternoon when she parked on top of a small hill and piled from her rig, grabbed a small pack from the back of the truck, and waved Lou to come along.

Stream pointed with one finger. "I camped right there for four days."

Then she pointed over the edge and down the slope to the bottom. "That body is down there. Given what I have been told, he died while I was still here." She frowned. "And I never heard a thing."

She started down toward the three people she could see just standing around, sipping coffee from their containers, waiting for her.

As she approached, one of them said, "He is kinna messy."

Stream walked toward the brush that he was pointing at.

The body was sprawled on its back, head aimed downhill. It was a mess all right.

The man's throat was ripped out. Whatever had gotten to him, it had not made a sound. She would have heard any kind of scream that close to where she had been sleeping, or sitting around relaxing during the day.

The pistol on his hip still had the safety strap in place.

One of the men held a plastic bag which her shoved in her direction.

"What'cha got, Pete?"

"Walll, Stream, it sure looks like one of those things that hospitals use to inject yur butt with when yur not looking. Afta we get this back to the lab we'll be able to tell you what is still in it. It is still loaded with somethin'."

He nodded at her. "Pretty strange thing to be totting around out here."

"Certainly is." She knelt and took a careful look at the dead guy's face, gasped, then looked up and over at Lou.

"It's our missing visitor. No wonder the other guy left in such a hurry. Whatever happened out here, he must have been around here somewhere and saw it happen."

Pete nodded and pointed. "Up top over yonder. We found where they were, left quite a trampled spot. Must have beena day or two."

His arm swivelled. "We also found tire tracks thata way, comin' and goin' from one of those old jeep tracks. From where they parked, two pair of boot prints comin' and one pair goin'. The wind messed up most of them but we saw enough to be able to say that."

Pete laughed. "From what we found up yonder they weren't exactly outdoors folk who camped a lot. You can inspect the debris later. We bagged it all and sent it in."

"Thanks, Pete. We're done. Thanks for waiting on us."

"No problem. See ya later, Stream."

She beckoned to Lou and started back up the steep slope to where she had parked, walking behind him.

"I really don't like the sounds of that. Not even a little bit."

He sighed loudly, stopped, and looked down at her.

"It sounds like they were after you. Not good, not good at all."

"Indeed. I think something that Fergy was up to will give us a hint. There was lots of stuff from his place and still plenty to go through. Ought to be something in all that."

The next day, she headed away from her place and after a somewhat short drive, parked, and banged into the office of a Wildlife Biologist that she knew. It said that on his outside door, *Wildlife Biologist*.

He looked up from whatever he had been reading and crunched his round face into a wide grin that stretched across his face, shoving the bags under his eyes upward, just a little. His face was the type of weathered face one gets after years and years of being assaulted by all kinds of weather. He was now sixty, or as he often stated, sixty, more or less, but probably quite a bit more than less.

"Heya, Stream!"

He waggled one hand toward the coffee maker on one of the low bookcases.

"Help yourself. And," he laughed happily, "what do you want to know this time?"

She filled a cup, took a seat, a sip, and winked at him.

Then she described that area she had just left, and asked, "What is wandering around out there that can, or would, rip out a man's throat so fast that he wouldn't have time to scream and that wouldn't make a sound doing it, probably at night?"

"Oh, ah, um ha?"

Wally Vinderal stared into a space only he could see as his mind sorted through all the data that happened to exist relative to the asked question.

"No sound," he mumbled. "Not many things would attack totally silently. Most would give an intruder some sort of warning threat sound first. Yee ha! Give them time to back away. Ummm ha."

"Trained guard dog might fit," he suggested.

"Wild not domestic," she stated.

"Wild?" His eyes refocused as he looked into her eyes. "Wild?"

"Right."

"Predator, then?"

"Why I asked."

Wally leaned back in his chair, picked up his large and never to be washed coffee cup, and took a sip.

"Mountain lion could. They can be very, very quiet when stalking prey. So, Cougar is one, maybe."

"What else?"

"Eh. Not a bear, that's for sure." He took a sip. "Wolves hunt in packs. I suppose a bunch could jump someone if they thought it was something slow, especially at night, perhaps. If someone was hunkered down their profile might fool the wolves into thinking it was their usual prey and if the breeze was blowing away from them toward the whatever."

He shrugged. "There really aren't a lot of large predators anywhere, top of the food chain and all that. And, unlike Florida, we don't have lots of escaped exotics on the loose to worry about. So, that's it, cougar or wolf."

He watched her expression. "Any tracks?"

"No, the wind did them in."

"Too bad." He took another sip. "Anything else you want to know?"

"Could it be a solitary wolf?"

"Maybe. A young male searching for a mate, one that left the pack. Although we have no record of anything like that ever happening, wolf attack like that."

Stream stood, walked over to the small sink and washed her cup and hung it on a peg.

"Well, thanks, again."

"Always a pleasure. Come over for dinner some time, soon. Wife is always happy to see you and is nagging me about things like that."

"I'll do that."

Cat In A Tree

Stream and Lou had spent two weeks putting together a thick report based on everything that had been learned from all the Fergy information.

When they had finished, finally, copies of the report were delivered to several varieties of law enforcement.

The end result, after many discussions over who would do what and who would get credit for what were resolved, was that an even dozen folk were hauled off to various lockups and held without bail which astonished those being locked up and outraged their attorneys who wept copious amounts of crocodile tears and then began to create reams of paper to oppose everything their fertile imagination could think off.

A large number of astonishingly large bank account were frozen both locally and elsewhere.

The shock waves of all this activity pulsated along the organization arteries, traveling ever upward, telling of what had happened to the unfortunate dozen who owned allegiance to that organization.

Stream dragged Lou off on a camping trip into the way beyond.

As they set up their primitive camp she suggested that it was a case of out of sight, out of mind, and that was the operating principle for the moment.

The spot that she had hauled him to was close to the edge of a great cliff that ran for miles in either direction. From here one could look out at lots and lots of quiet and emptiness, empty that is, of people. There were plenty of other living things out there creeping, crawling, walking, and flying about.

"Well, what do you think?" she asked as the sun rose from behind them on their second day and as she dumped breakfast onto their tin plates.

Lou took a forkfull, chewed thoughtfully, nodded, and said, "Pretty good."

"Not the food, being out here."

He smiled at her. "Pretty good. Also."

She hissed at him and refilled their cups from the pan where the coffee grounds had been boiled.

He took a careful sip from the steaming beverage. Set the cup down, stretched and yawned. "Pretty good. AGAIN!"

Then he winked at her.

"Feels good. Being out here. The job is finished. Feels good."

She laughed.

"Ummmmm?"

"What?"

Lou looked out at the view as the sun began to light everything in sight.

"How did this outfit ever come into existence? It operates in a way that would cause any cop shop or attorney's office great heartburn and would send them running screaming in the opposite direction."

She shrugged.

"The boss has never told anyone how he did it, exactly. But I do know that he yanked on some rather big strings, for money, connections, and general all around arm twisting, and very heavy political pressure."

"Of course," she added, "after we produced results and gave it all to the appropriate places and faded carefully into the background, folk began to see the utility of our work as well as the results, all credit going to them not us."

She grinned. "And in spite of how it looks, everything that we do is absolutely legal as it can get. Just unorthodox on the face of it."

Lou looked at her, frowning, eyes squinting down into narrow slits.

"Stream, you have got to be careful. You already have had burglars, an attempted assassination, and now we have bagged a whole bunch of nogoodnicks that have been around for a long time, hiding in plain sight. These guys, those guys, are going to get pretty angry, and pretty angry bad guys tend to get wild and erratic."

She nodded and refilled their coffee cups.

"Noted, noted, noted. However, assistant mine, I am careful, I just don't look worried."

She waggled a hand at their surroundings.

"Anyone that wants to sneak up on us out here had better use a hot air balloon."

She winked at him.

"And if this place gets visited, I know a place where we can camp that anyone trying to enter will probably break one or more legs, at least, if they don't get killed in the process."

She stood.

"Let's take a little hike."

The week passed surrounded by the quiet of the outdoors, the time spent relaxing, and taking little hikes.

On the fourth day, the day before they would return to "civilization," while on a little hike, Stream stopped and pointed toward the direction they had come from.

"Listen. Carefully."

Lou did.

"A truck? Coming this way?"

She nodded.

"Uh huh. They are at least a full hour away. Driving that jeep track cannot be done in a rush. Plenty of time for us to get back to meet and greet whoever it is."

The hike back was less than casual.

Stream opened a side panel in the back of her truck and dragged out a large metal case.

Setting it on the ground, she popped the latches

And opened the case.

A pair of large pistols set in snug padding gleamed soft metal shine at them. Along one edge of the case, equally well padded, were a number of small boxes.

She took out one weapon, one box, and began to load her choice.

Lou pulled out the other and began to do the same thing.

"You a good shot?"

"Good enough." He checked his weapon and stuffed it in the small of his back.

Stream pulled her shirt loose, shoved her weapon in the front of her trousers, and draped the shirt over it.

She sat, started the small stove, and began to reheat the coffee.

"Wonder who's coming?" She set a spoon near the stove. "Work knows where we are and how to get here. Other than that?" She shrugged.

By the time that the truck arrived, they were standing, not too close to each other, not to far way, coffee cups held in their left hands, right arms dangling loose.

"Gimble gob," grumbled Stream. "It is one of our's." She sighed. "Now what?"

A tall, slim woman stepped from the truck, cow-girl comfortable, old jeans, old boots, old denim shirt.

"Hey, Stream."

"Fran," replied Stream. "A long drive. We would have been back tomorrow."

Fran nodded.

She held out an envelope.

"The boss wants you to have this. Take some time to think about it. No hurry back."

She turned and walked back to her truck, smiled, and waved. "See ya."

She slipped into the still running truck and headed back the way she had come.

Stream opened the envelope, took out a single sheet of folded paper, opened it, and read.

"Crap and then some," she growled. She handed it to Lou.

He stared at it. It was a drawing of a tree with a cat in it, way near the top, looking down. The artist's signature curved in a wild scrawl around the base of the tree. It was a piece of art worth framing.

"What?" he asked.

"We drive back tomorrow. Saturday we get clean, eats lots of good food, and rest much."

"Sunday, we go visit." She took back the sheet of paper, folded it, and replaced it in the envelope. She winked at him. "You'll see."

Then she nudged him with her shoulder.

"You will stay at my place. Ummmm, keep the gun."

She kicked a small rock to one side.

"Let's take a hike."

Lou nodded.

Mid-morning, Sunday, Lou walked into her kitchen wearing a gigantic towel.

"Very Greek," she observed as she waggled a hand at several pans. "Have some breakfast, surfer dude."

He sat at the table, carefully tucking his towel into place, and began to fill his plate.

"Where's my clothes?"

"Taking a joy ride in the drier." She looked at the clock over the stove. "Umm, be ready in about ten minutes, heavy sleeper."

She was wearing a pair of bright blue pajamas, feet encased in fluffy slippers.

"You eat, I'll get dressed, and then check on your duds. They'll be nice and warm."

She headed down the hall, dropping most of the accumulated mail in the trash can.

He could see the outline of the large gun in her side pocket.

By the time he was done with breakfast and pouring another cup of coffee, Stream entered the kitchen from a different door, and set a stack of neatly folded clothes in front of him.

"Here you go, Tiger. Get dressed. We are going to visit." She walked toward the living room.

Lou headed to one of the spare bedrooms, draped his towel over the top of the door, and quickly dressed. Everything was nice and warm.

Then he headed for the living room, gun in his jacket pocket.

Far across town, in an area of rather modest looking houses that had lots of open space between them, Stream pulled into a driveway and parked in front of one, nicely painted, white with pale blue trim around the door and windows.

She strode up to the front door and tried the knob.

"Locked!"

Stream kicked the bottom of the door with a boot tip.

"OPEN UP!"

"Meow, meow, meow," purred a voice from the speaker mounted above the door.

"Co . . . han," she snarled as she kicked the door four more times, each harder than the last.

"Cohan, open the damn door!"

Lou heard several electric locks pop and unlatch.

Stream opened the door and stepped inside the short hall, shutting the door behind Lou as he entered.

The locks latched.

"Ahhhhhh," said the voice of someone out of sight, "we are being visited by the ever so delightful Stream with her stud side-kick. Do come in."

Lou looked at her. She shrugged.

And led him into a large windowless room, and turned to the right.

A very large man sat comfortably slouched in a

large plush chair.

Lou figured him to be about six feet six inches or so, heavy but not fat. He was either American Indian, or, some Asiatic non-Chinese, judging by his facial features.

"Cohan, this is Lou." She dropped into a chair. "What do you want?"

Lou sat in a middle chair from which he could watch the both of them.

"Want, Sweetling? Nothing, nada. Nothing but to have a chit chat."

"Sooooooo?" she drawled.

Cohan rose to his feet, a very careful, choreographic production of standing up.

Lou now figured him to be six feet, eight inches, at least.

"I," stated Cohan, "in spite of the early hour, am going to have a wee bit of this or that." He smiled at them. "Actually more than a mere wee bit. Would you like something? Coffee? Tea? Other?"

"Coffee," stated Stream. "For two. Black."

"Most certainly." Cohan flowed from the room, all graceful movement.

"Who is this guy?" whispered Lou.

"I'll explain later," she murmured back.

Cohan returned, bearing a very large tray which held a coffee container, two large cups, and a bottle of some liquid that glittered in the light.

He set the coffee container on a small table

between Stream and Lou, handed each of them a cup, and took the bottle in one hand and sailed the tray to one side where it landed on the middle cushion of a large couch.

Settling in his chair, Cohan took a long pull from his bottle, opened in his kitchen. He didn't bother with a glass.

He held out the bottle and sloshed the contents back and forth.

"RUM, BY GUM! The drink of Pirates and that sort of ilk. Yo, ho, ho, ho, etc."

He took another swallow, set the bottle on the floor beside his chair, and leaned toward Stream.

"And, as we were just speaking of Pirates, my dear one, that is the problem. You just put a bunch of them in the slammer. Stream, you are in great danger. You have done something to it that hasn't happened before. Beware, talented child warrior, beware!" His eyes swivelled to Lou, his gaze seemed to bore into Lou's eyes.

"She is a great treasure, our Stream, one that must be protected, one that must be allowed to do all that she has chosen to do. Gird your loins, strong one. Take up your weapons, you will have terrible and bloody work to do."

Cohan leaned back, snatched up his bottle from the floor, and emptied it in one very long swallow. Then he smiled at her.

"So, how goes everything with you?"

You've Got To Be Kidding

Ztrich sat in his modestly sized office furnished with modest furniture and over his modest desk at the pair that sat in the modest chairs facing him.

He took a sip from his coffee cup and nodded at the one that looked at ease, the other twitched every so often.

James L. took a sip from his cup and indicated the other man.

"This is Samuel Anabail. He and his very long term partner, Henry "Hank" Winton, were the for-hire guys that I sent to watch and to see to that lady special investigator." He took another sip and looked at Samuel.

"Tell Z everything that you told me, every detail, leave nothing out. He has to hear it directly and unedited from you."

James L. slumped in his chair and wondered how Z was going to react when he heard what Samuel had to say. It was kinna hard to believe.

Samuel started, starting from the moment he and Hank had been hired and what his latest instructions from James L. had been.

Z looked at James L.

"You decided to eliminate her?"

James L. nodded.

"Continue," said Z, waggling one hand at Samuel.

Samuel very carefully narrated his tale, making sure that every detail was correct. When he finished, his face was wet with sweat and a few tears.

Ztrich's eyes looked from the shaking Samuel to the calm James L. who then added everything that had happened "down there" since.

Z stared at him.

"You've got to be kidding!"

James L. shook his head.

"No, Z, not at all. It is all true!"

Z sat up and stared even harder at his number one and long time friend.

"Dogs killed some clumsy burglars and a large dog got Hank?"

James L. nodded.

"And the cops hauled away everybody based on solid evidence?"

James L. nodded, again.

Ztrich leaned back and slid open a desk drawer, and reached into it. Samuel blanched. Z hauled out a very thick envelope and held it out to Samuel.

"Here, Samuel, take a long, a very long, a year long vacation. Talk to us when you get back."

Samuel took the envelope, nodded, stood, and

left the office.

"Fergy?"

James L. nodded.

"Probably," he said. "We know that everything about him was being investigated. It is too late to close that barn door."

Z nodded.

"Any ideas about that so-called "special" investigator?" he asked.

James L. shook his head.

"Not at the moment. The newspapers didn't say much about anything. Nothing was mentioned, other than the fact about the dogs, eh, in both cases."

"That is a strange place down there."

James L. nodded.

"Lots and lots of open space down there. The investigator apparently spends many days a year wandering around in it. So she probably has a good idea of how not to get eaten by the wild life."

"Not exactly an urban dweller is she?"

"Nope."

"We know anything more about her?"

"Nope. Someone really messed around with the records down there."

"Interesting. Feds?"

James L. shrugged.

"I think," suggested Z, "that we leave that neck of the woods alone from some time."

"Sure."

James L. emptied his coffee cup, set it on the edge of the desk, and left.

Ztrich swung his chair around and looked out his window. It was a fairly nice day out there, no rain.

So, What'da'ya Know?

Lou and Stream were relaxing in her living room, tall glasses, filled with a golden liquid that sparkled as the light passed through it, in hand. They were talking and taking a small sip now and then.

The bottle had arrived by messenger from Cohan.

"Go easy with that stuff, Lou. It will dissolve your bones."

He nodded. "I believe that." And took another cautious sip.

Stream had cooked chicken in a red sauce loaded with chilies and other spices that she felt like tossing into the pot. It was served with dumplings and boiled potatoes, a bean dish, and corn tortillas.

Stream slumped deeper in her chair and took another sip. Lou was sitting on the floor, leaning back against an overstuffed chair.

"Everything that has been happening," she said, "reminds me of the opening of a program that I listen to every once in awhile on National Public Radio."

"It does?"

"Yep. The program always opens with the host

asking the audience, So what'da'ya know? And they always reply, not much, you? And from what's happening that is exactly how I feel. I don't know much about much of anything."

She slid slowly from her chair and thumped to the floor.

"OOOF! I think that damn seer is up to no good."

"Who?" Lou squinted at her.

"Cohan."

"Oh. Seer?"

She nodded.

"Bad translation," she explained. "It is the best approximation. He is from one of the tribes, he refuses to say which, but that is what he is. The actual term means something like the one who sees/knows things that all us normal folk can't. That was what his drawing was all about."

Lou took a sip.

"That cat in the tree?"

"Yep. It said that I was in danger."

"Huh?"

"Cats run up trees when danger threatens."

"Oh. He could have just written."

She laughed.

"Never happen." She took a sip. "Ummmm, I think I am getting used to this stuff. Or, it has burned all my taste buds away. It has been a long time since he sent over a bottle of this stuff. I kinna forgot. He is wealthy, is Cohan. His paintings and drawings, when he puts one on the market, cause a bidding frenzy among a certain bunch of collectors."

"Ah." Lou wobbled his head. "I think that this stuff has numbed my chin."

"Don't drink any more!"

"Glass is empty."

"Well then, at least you are already on the floor, not far to fall."

"Crap," grumbled Lou.

"Cohan therapy," explained Stream.

"Oh. Then I suppose that it is working."

She giggled. "Have no fear, it won't have a lasting effect."

"Good to hear." Lou leaned back against the front of his chair and squinted hard at her, eyes mere slits. She was beginning to get difficult to see.

"You look," he slurred, "pretty nice, all fuzzy and out of focus."

"Only?"

"Nope, boss-o-roo. It was worse in bright daylight. Dazzling, overpowering. You know that, don't you?"

She stared at him, took another sip, and slumped a little bit more.

"Never had anyone mumble such a thing to me before. Nope-o-roo."

"Just," hissed Lou, softly, "leave my body where it falls." He canted sideways in a loose limbed sprawl, sound asleep.

Stream lurched to her feet and bumped into the couch, dragged the afghan from it and tossed it in his general direction, and toppled onto the couch. She was successful in that she managed to get most of herself on it.

"Damn that Cohan," she slurred into sleep.

Sun beams were crawling across the living room when her eyes opened, more or less.

Staring up at the ceiling, she told herself, "That was a really bad idea."

Rolling from the couch she managed to stand and lurched toward the kitchen and the refrigerator.

Dragging out the container of orange juice, she drank half of it, started the coffee maker, pre-filled last night early on.

As it burbled and bubbled, she sat at the kitchen table, elbows propped on top of it, hands holding her head.

Someone opened the front door and came into the kitchen.

"There is a dead body in your living room."

"Not quite, Lupe. Why are you here?"

Lupe opened the refrigerator, took out numbers of items, and began to prepare breakfast.

"Grandmother was worried. You didn't go to work at your usual time nor did you go anywhere else."

"Tell her thank you for the concern. Just having a little R'n'R, a liquid R'n'R courtesy of Cohan."

Lupe shook her head. "You ought to know better."

"Do. But it is sneaky stuff. Forgot."

Lupe pointed toward the living room. "Will your assistant survive?"

"Little early to tell but I think so. If not, it will be hard to explain it to the boss."

Something growled in the living room.

Stream looked up. "Sounds like he did. Make lots. Going to take a lot to recover."

Lupe chopped up a number of chillies and dumped them into whatever it was that she was doing with the eggs.

Lou made it to the kitchen door and stood there, one hand clenching to door jamb.

"That orange juice?" he croaked.

"Yep. Sit. Have some."

Stream filled a large glass and shoved it across the table top at an empty chair.

He dropped into the chair and drained the glass.

"What is that stuff made from?"

"Unknown," said Stream.

"Secret," added Lupe.

"We are not going to work today," stated Stream. "Don't need those bloodshot eyes bleeding all over our documents."

"Huh." Lou poured more orange juice into his glass and eyed the food that Lupe was setting on the table.

"Eat it," ordered Lupe. "It is good for you."

She headed for the front door.

"I will tell Grandmother that everything is all right."

"Thanks, Lupe," mumbled Stream, her mouth full.

When she finished her breakfast, she carefully walked into the hall.

"Stay there. Be back in awhile."

Lou heard the shower start, running hard. It ran for quite some time, then stopped.

Stream walked into the kitchen wearing a thick terry cloth robe, a towel wrapped around her head and her hair. She poured a cup of coffee, dumped in some sugar, and sat at the table. She pointed at the hallway.

"Anytime that you wish, or are able. The shower is that away. Look for the steam."

She took a swallow from her cup and nodded.

"Ahhhhh, feeling better. The after effects wear off pretty fast."

Lou stood, slowly unbent, turned, and headed down the hall.

Stream smiled and took another swallow from her cup.

Lou eventually returned wearing another of those gigantic towels.

"Couldn't find one of those robes."

She shoved a filled cup over to him.

"Looking better already."

He took a swallow.

"Thanks."

She stood, fetched the coffee pot, refilled both their cups, then washed it and reloaded it and started a new pot.

"You don't look to bad fuzzy and out of focus yourself." She sat and winked at him.

"Argh! You remembered that. Sorry."

"It was . . . nice, strange but nice. Nothing to worry about, partner."

He stared at her.

"Did you treat all your assistants like this?"

"Nope. Nary a one. You are a special case."

He jerked. "I am?"

"For now it is just a sorta hunch. But you are doing just fine. As the fishermen would say, you are a keeper."

He smiled weakly at her, not at all sure what she was implying.

"If I survive."

She laughed.

"Look, Lou, my previous assistants were always getting upset by this or that, they wanted everything to be nice and orderly and regular, understandable behavior. You just go along with whatever is happening or whatever I might decide we need to do. I doubt any of the others could have handled a visit to Cohan. He would have twisted them around badly and scared them off. He saw something in you, Lou. Hence, his little gift."

She took another swallow from her cup and held it high and toward him.

"Congratulations!"

"Huh?"

"You can work with me as long as you wish to be, or can stand to be." She grinned at him. "And you are pretty good company, ummm, as well."

She stood.

"Feel like a slow walk around the neighborhood?"

"Sure. I'll go get dressed."

She grinned at him.

"What?"

"Good idea. I don't think anyone around here would believe that you are a Greek that is visiting and wearing your native garb."

So they took a slow walk around the neighborhood as soon as he got dressed.

As they wandered along, Stream pointed out that there were no curbs or sidewalks. The outside walls of all the properties edged the road.

"This section is a very, very old part of town, more or less the original part."

She kicked the surface of the road. There was a great patch of cobblestone showing where the asphalt had failed.

"Original road, lasts a lot longer than that stuff."

After a long circuit during which Stream had

suggested to Lou that rumpled and crumpled looking clothes weren't all that unusual in this area, she pointed at a place as they approached her home.

"The Grandmother's house from hence have come my house watchers and personal worry butts."

She unlocked her gate, shoved it open, and closed it after him as he entered.

"Not going to lock it?"

"Nope." She led him into the living room.

And looked around.

"Help me straighten up this place. Rala, the Squirrel, is coming for lunch."

He began to do as ordered.

"Uh?"

"I want to ask her about anything that she found that was not local. Our report only dealt with the local crooks. I have a bad feeling that there are others out there."

She began to set the kitchen table for lunch.

"Ah, Lou?" she called.

"Ummm?"

"Let me set the conversational pace. We will get to her research eventually and the questions that I want to ask."

"Sure." He stuck his head into the kitchen. "I am gonna take a quicky nap before then."

He walked back to the large couch and sprawled flat on his back and fell asleep.

Finished with the lunch preparation, Stream

headed for her bedroom to take a nap as well. Rala had keys to everything and could let herself in.

During lunch Rala told them all about a movie she had just watched, DVD, and about the various characters, the actors, and the story line.

Once lunch and her telling were finished, Stream served them coffee, tea for Rala, and asked her the questions.

Rala set quietly for a long time.

Lou frowned.

Stream winked at him. It was normal. For Rala. She was processing all the data that she could recall. Finally she smiled at Stream.

Stream waited.

Rala told them.

A Question

Ztrich sat in his modestly sized office and stared across his modest desk at his two most senior staff and long-time friends sitting in the modest chairs, facing him.

No one was slouching. This was a very serious meeting, much more serious that any meeting they had held here in a very, very long time.

Z checked that all the coffee cups were full: his cup, James' cup, and Ralph's cup.

"It is like a cancer," stated Ralph. "It started down there in the boonies and has spread to a number of other places."

James L. nodded, took a sip, and said, "I have a very bad feeling that this is, somehow, linked to Fergy."

Z sipped from his cup, and nodded at him. It was a proceed nod.

"Fergy was always a solo act. He was forever boasting that he kept everything in his head, no written records. That is why we brought him into the organization."

James L. looked at his boss for a long time, then he continued.

"I think that Fergy was very unhappy about that, being brought into the organization, or became very unhappy about that. I think that he began to keep records, very detailed records, and that is where all this is coming from. Whoever emptied his place got all those records and is using them."

Z looked at him.

"Any way we can get all those records back?"

Ralph sighed.

"Z, we can't even get our hands on what all those law folk are using. They have managed, somehow, to get some fancy court order to keep it all hidden. All of them have managed to finagle the Feds to see it as some sort of National Security something or other. It gives them a very free hand to do whatever they are doing."

Z refilled his cup and the two carefully held out others.

"Who," he asked, " is the source? Who is feeding them all that info?"

James L. set his cup on the desk top.

"I think that it started in the boonies. That is where we lost people to," he wiggled his fingers in the air, "dog attacks, and where Fergy lived, and died."

Z nodded.

"O.K., here is what you two will do. Each one, independently, will hire the best researchers money can get. Regardless of the cost." He handed each of them a single sheet of paper. This is a list of the things I, we, want to know. Use as many people as you think is necessary."

Z cleared his throat. "I want to know each and every tidbit as they are found, bring that to me, right away, and don't stop until I tell you."

He waggled one hand at them.

"In two days, let me know how things are going."

The pair stood, and left the office, holding their own sheet of paper, heading for their offices.

Z sighed, pulled a sheet of paper from his desk drawer, and began to make another list.

Wake Not A Sleeping Wolf

It had been a rather quite two weeks.

Lou and Stream had written a number of reports on this small matter or that small matter. All in all, it was rather quiet as things in her office usually went.

Lou was still being Lou. He was still somewhat uncertain about her and still tended to be leery about almost everything. Although he did seem, to her way of thinking, to be getting less and less that way.

Stream was just being Stream. She dragged him to whatever popped into her mind, from the dingy to the most elegant, restaurants and art galleries. It was, as she thought of it, a necessary activity as he seemed sorta isolated from various cultural aspects of life.

And so it went, day after day after day after day.

Now they were in the process of finishing lunch in a place that Lou hadn't been taken to before. It was neither dingy nor elegant, just a small and comfortable place to have lunch.

The owner had greeted Stream with a great bear hug and then almost literally dragged her to the table that he thought was the one where she ought to be seated.

The dessert had been a surprise to Lou. It had been a taste sensation of cake and frosting. Over coffee, he puzzled over exactly what the cook had used to create such a concoction.

While they sat is quiet comfort, drinking coffee, the front door banged open, the door thumping against the wall. A messenger ran into the place, eyes quickly scanning the few customers, and ran to their table. He shoved an envelope at Stream, turned and ran from the place.

Lou stared in the direction the messenger had raced and then at the envelope she was holding.

"What was that?"

Stream opened it, took out a sheet of paper, looked at it, and then sat absolutely still.

As Lou started to say something, she shoved the sheet of paper at him without saying a word.

Lou took it and frowned.

It was another Cohan drawing.

Running up the center of the sheet was a tall dead twisted tree, jagged bare arms stretching to either side. About two thirds of the way from the bottom, a large bird of some sort sat far out of a horizontal limb holding a sheet of paper in its beak. The sheet dangled past a number of the lower limbs. It had writing in an elegant script on it.

Double, double, toil and trouble,
Fire burn and cauldron bubble.

By the prickling on my thumbs,
Something wicked this way comes.

Flee! Stream!
Your parents need you.
Your property is safe.

He looked across the table at her and handed her the sheet.

Stream, surged to her feet, tossed some bills on the table.

"Let's go, partner. There is no time to waste."

She hurried from the restaurant and toward her truck.

As soon as he jumped in, she started down the street, just a wee bit over the legal limit. Lou put the folded sheet in the glove box.

"My place first. We'll load all my gear then go to your place. Take only rugged and heavy duty clothes and boots."

Once they were inside her house, she led him to the correct room and began to point out at the things to take.

"Hurry, Lou, hurry."

She dashed down the hall to the kitchen, picked the phone and hit a button.

"Hi, boss. Triple security on everyone, 24/7. I'll be gone for some unknown amount of time. Will explain when I return. Take no prisoners."

She hung up, dragged over a step stool and opened one of the high cabinet doors and took out two cardboard boxes. Blowing the dust from them, she set them on the kitchen table and then began to pile food next to the boxes from several other cabinets. She hurried away and back again holding a number of empty boxes and began to stuff the food into them.

Lou had hurried and gotten all their gear loaded in her truck.

Now they were headed across town. As they left her place, Lou looked back at her open gate.

"Don't worry about it," she said. "It will be taken care of."

"Ummm?"

"What?"

"Is going on?" she said, finishing his sentence for him.

"Yep."

"Cohan's warning. We're heading up to the Pacific Northwest to where my parents live and where I grew up."

"Any idea?"

"Nope. Those two cardboard boxes with the blue tape contained money, lots of it. We are, now and until we return, on a cash economy. No triggers, no trace."

She pointed at the maps sitting on the hump between the seats.

"I marked the route, all two lane roads, for the

most part. You are the navigator."

He opened the top map.

"All small roads?"

"Mostly. No one can watch all those roads. Folk mainly watch the freeways which tend to funnel most of the traffic through spots that are easily watched."

She grinned over at him, just a quick glance from the road ahead.

"You bring your pistola?"

"Yep."

"Good."

Eventually as the day was turning to dim, she turned into a narrow side road and into a National Forest campground. She circled around, inspecting all the open spots and the few folk already camped, and parked.

"Good place," she announced. Jumping out, she open a bag of tools laying in the back of the truck and selected the proper one and began to take off the rear license plate and replace it with another. Then she walked around to the front and did the same thing.

Standing, she pointed. "Go get an envelope from up there. Bring it back. They want your license plate number and state."

She laughed as he started off to fetch the registration envelope. "Now, as of this moment, we are from California."

Lou returned shortly and filled in the blanks on the envelope.

"How many days?"

"Just the one." She handed him the necessary money. "We will be on the road in the morning."

And they were, right after breakfast, they were on the road, trending ever onward toward the Pacific Northwest.

The environment slowly changed and became more mountains and forests and less open space.

Late in the afternoon they were now driving through low hills and open grassy areas on either side of the road.

"This is all Bureau of Land Management land, for the most part. We'll turn at the next place, at the next opening. Then it is just a short drive until we are out of sight of the road. There we'll camp.

They did. Other than the faint sound of a stray vehicle passing by back on the two-lane road they had just left, it was very quiet. They were alone. No one else had chosen to drive back here and camp.

"Weathers nice," observed Stream. "We won't need to put up a tent. This is an early camp, get a little loafing time in. Tomorrow will be a long drive. We will arrive fairly late at our destination."

As she began to make dinner, Lou asked, "Aren't you worried about those license plates?"

"Nope. Not at all. They're good."

"Oh?"

"Yep. They belong to the sister of this truck. Both were bought at the same time from the same dealer. She lives on a small farm of a friend. He pays the license fees as they come due and sends me the tags. If necessary, I send him the plates, and then he sends them back. So, if any busy body checks on them they will find out that the address is correct and all that. The envelope in the glove box has the registration and a notarized document that says that I can drive the truck anywhere, signed by the owner."

She grinned at him. "I have a valid California driver's license as well."

Lou shook his head.

"What?"

"Exactly what kind of outfit do you, do we, work for?"

She shrugged. "Just one that wishes for all its folks to not be bothered by nosey people, that's all. We provide a valuable service to various law enforcement agencies by doing research which we give to them, no strings attached. So, they are happy. Most of them don't have the resources to allow their folk to spend all the time we do."

"O.K."

"Sure?"

"Yep." He watched her finish cooking and dump a large quantity into each of the tin plates.

"Here you go, partner. Not too bad, but filling."

When they finished and cleaned up things, she taught him how to play cribbage. Stream had brought along the board and everything one needed for the game.

Even though he lost two games out of three, he smiled, and said, "I like this game."

"Good." She nodded as she put everything back into its case.

"Light's getting dim." She pointed. "You go that way, I will head this way. Do what you need to do. It's early to bed and early to rise."

She stood and headed in her chosen direction.

In the twilight of early morning they ate, packed, and were on their way.

As was their custom on this trip, she only stopped for gas. Lou was in charge of making sandwiches from the materials they had brought along. They ate these on the road.

By noon they were crossing the rather desolate environment that was the southern part of Idaho driving at five miles over the speed limit on the freeway.

Stream was determined to arrive at her parent's place before it got too dark outside, or at least, fairly early in the evening.

They arrived in the last dusk of a summer day. The last portion of the drive was slower as the long dirt mountain road wandered through dense forest until they drove out into a large open meadow surrounded by very tall pine and other species of the local area. She parked next to the house sitting at the far edge of that meadow.

A woman was sitting on the swing on the front porch, slowly rocking back and forth.

She stopped, stood, and came down the wooden stairs.

Her skin was a soft brown, her eyes black as her hair.

"Welcome home, daughter," she said as she hugged her.

Once she was released, Stream told her, "This is my partner, Lou. Partner at work."

"Inside you two, my husband is just finishing dinner and is right now putting it on the table. You can probably use a good meal after your trip."

As Lou trailed them inside the house he felt his mouth began to salivate as the odors of dinner assaulted his nostrils.

"Smells really, really good." He felt extremely hungry.

Stream's mother pointed. "You may wash in there, if you wish."

Lou headed in the correct direction, washed his hands and face, then followed the sounds of soft conversation and the clattering of dinner plates being set in place.

A tall, slim man smiled at him and indicated a chair at the table. "Sit here, Lou."

And as soon as the others sat in their places, he said, "Help yourself to whatever is close and then pass it to your left." He took a large scoop of mashed potatoes and handed the bowl to Stream, who sat to his left. Then he ladled gravy over them and set that bowl in front of her.

Lou dragged a platter close to his plate.

"Turkey and German sausage," explained her father. "Take whatever you wish. I will have both."

The plates were large but soon filled with some of everything on the table.

The conversation, and the questions, were as gentle as the parent's voices.

Once the dessert was demolished, a smooth as silk cheese cake, they moved to the living room where her father filled tall glasses with a light brown liquid.

"Made locally. Some folks got licensed to make whiskey."

He took a swallow and then looked at Stream.

"So, daughter. Why are you here? I can tell that this is not just a social call, a long past due social call."

She shook her head.

Then she looked at her mother who said, "Tell us."

Then her eyes wandered from parent to parent.

"I have been warned, twice, of a great danger. I came up here to protect you from it."

Her mother glanced at her father and said, "It is as I said."

He nodded.

Stream stared at them. "You were expecting me?"

"It is so," replied her mother.

"How did you know?" whispered Stream.

Her father nodded at his wife.

"The wolves told me," she stated.

She pointed toward the outside. "There are three packs that have drifted into this area from Montana and Wyoming areas over the years."

"The . . . wolves . . . told . . . you?"

"Most so," replied her mother. "They have been singing for the past three nights."

She took a swallow from her glass.

"Even the song dogs, who fear the wolves, came close enough to sing the same message."

"Wolves and coyotes?" asked Stream.

"It is so."

She pointed. "When the moon is there, we will sit on the porch swing and you will tell me everything."

Stream nodded.

Dark eyes watched her face carefully and turned to Lou.

"What is your full and true name, warrior?"

Lou blinked and took a sip from his glass.

"Lucien," he said. "Lucien Prince Woulfe. That is wolf ending in a 'e' which is silent. It is pronounced wolf, not wolf-ee, or wolf-eh."

Her mother nodded at him and looked at Stream.

"Hee ya! Daughter we have much to discuss, yes we do." She pointed at the hall. "Lou, you may have the bedroom, first door on the left side. Stream knows where her's is. Both are made up for occupation."

She smiled at them.

"Now we will speak of small town happenings and things like that."

And soon, Stream sat on the porch in the swing with her mother while her father "entertained" Lou in the kitchen. Stream could tell that her father was very curious about this fella that she had dragged along home. It had never happened before.

Her mother slowly pushed the swing back and forth.

"You know, talented daughter, that my ancestors have been around for a long, long time."

Stream nodded. "American Indian."

Her mother laughed. "Truly a nonsense term. We are not American anything. We are the original immigrants. Sometime, ten, or fifteen, thousand years ago, we came to this continent. We were here long before a thing called America came into existence. We are Indians. For all those thousands of years we were Indians. Even though we were murdered into submission, the nonsense P.C. terms used today signify nothing except gross ignorance on the part of the folk who use them and who fail to recognize that we are the First People."

She patted her daughter's thigh.

"We are a different bunch than all those late comers. We see things differently, we think about things differently, and we do things differently."

She laughed softly.

"And that is why I wanted us to sit out here and so I could have a talk with my daughter."

"Why?"

"You do not bear any resemblance to your mother's genetic inheritance, other than you have dark hair. That Viking that I married has genes that made you look the way you are, one of the pale people, except for your beautiful black hair. Yet, you are so very much more."

Stream leaned sideways against her.

"I know."

"Not really."

"What do you mean?"

"Just listen now, no questions my ever curious child."

"O.K."

"When I knew that I was bearing you, my mother and her mother, came to visit. At that time, my mother's mother must have been in her nineties at least, no one was ever sure of her age, but she was somewhere around that."

"That Ancient One told my mother and they told me that you were a Special Child." She nudged Stream with an elbow. "Obviously you are one, by those other people's standards. You have a great imagination, you have a great curiosity, and you have a carefully hidden intelligence. There are all very fine attributes to have, you use them well. But, there is more. It is time for you to know that."

"More? What?"

Stream straightened up and looked at her.

"What more?"

Her mother smiled at her.

"In our peoples culture, at times, there are those that have abilities that allow them to see, or do, what most cannot. We do not worry about that, and we do not ostracize them. We just understand."

She waggled one hand toward the road entering the meadow from the forest. "All those other folk out there do not understand. They always talk of superstition, or conjuring tricks."

"My mother's mother was a Special Child. My mother was not. I am. In terms of this modern world, there must have been some type of genetic mutation long, long ago for new abilities that could passed on. I do not know of anyone who would do the proper research to truly know that. Suffice it to say that it does occur and one must accept whatever one is. From what my mother's mother told, it passes along the female line. But it does seems to skip generations in an unpredictable pattern. And as she told me, as she self-discovered, this ability is expressed when that female reaches a certain age."

She laughed softly. "Happy birthday, Stream daughter."

She kicked the swing back into motion.

"Tell me, daughter, have you experienced

strange, lately? Strange, as all those others would see it."

Stream nodded and told her.

A Small Adventure.

Stream walked across the broad meadow toward the game trail she knew exited over there and one that she knew very well.

The moon, over half-full, was coating everything in white light. There was certainly enough light for anyone to see where they were walking.

She had run and played in all directions from the house for hours uncounted during her childhood and up through high school. The knowledge of her surroundings out here were detailed enough that she could find her way from place to place in the near dark.

It took her parents a number of years to finally accept that she could do that and to stop worrying, or to least lower the fretting to a, more or less, comfortable level.

But, now, tonight, she was doing exactly as her mother had told her to do.

The game trail she now strode along would lead her, in its meandering way, to another meadow, a much smaller one, nestled inside thick forest.

She was told to stand in the center of this meadow and to wait, patiently, until the sun rose. Her mother told her that this way was a learning experience, one she had to experience, one where explanation would not be enough for her to understand.

So she strode through the dappled moonlight, listening intently to the sounds of the forest at night. Before she left, Stream had told Lou to not wait up, she would be safe doing what she had to do, and would see him when she returned.

He nodded, watched her stroll across the meadow and fade into the forest, then sat in the porch swing. He would wait here until she returned.

As she rounded the last bend in the game trail she could see the meadow grass shining in the moonlight, glowing soft silver. Walking to the center, the more or less center, she stood and began to wait, and closed her eyes to better hear the night sounds.

Taking slow, deep breathes, she relaxed, listening, reaching out with her sense of hearing, her sense of smell.

She stood and waited.
Nothing.
Nothing.
Nothing.

Something wet and cold touched her dangling right hand.

Her eyes flew open. Her head turned ever so slowly as she looked down.

A large dark colored wolf sat next to her, looking up at her. It was his nose that Stream had felt. As she looked around she could see that she was surrounded by large silent shadow shapes lying in the tall grass.

She hadn't heard or smelled them as they made their silent approach.

One by one, they stood, approached and sniffed her hand, then licked it, returning to their spot in the grass.

Now that, thought Stream, is interesting. But what do I do now?

Nothing, came the thought in her mind. She didn't have to do anything.

So, she stood, a silent figure, and looked around.

The wolves stood and walked away, drifting silent into the forest.

She stood and waited.
And waited.
And waited.

Then she saw forms that seem to materialize in a different sector of the meadow. They slipped through the tall grass toward her, stopped, and watched her.

It must be one of the other wolf packs, she mused to herself. Mother had said that there were three packs that had settled in this part of the state.

The pack around her seemed more attentive, ears held upright, heads swiveling here and there. Yet, each member cautiously approached, sniffed at one of her hands, and gave her a soft tongued lick.

Then she was alone almost before she realized the pack had departed.

She stood and waited.
And waited.
And waited.

Stream had decided that was what was going on, was some sort of wolf greeting.

As they did it, she realized what her mother had told her. She nodded to herself, somehow her mother knew this would happen if she came this deep into the forest to this specific meadow.

As she watched them, she thought, damn, I forgot to count them.

She closed her eyes and tried to visualize each of the packs as they came and went and to make her count that way. It didn't exactly work but she got a rough estimate of their number and wondered how many there really were.

Many, came the thought into her mind.

She opened her eyes and there they were, the third pack.

To her, in this light, the pack seemed to be a larger group than either of the first two.

Then she understood. This was the first pack to settle here, the first to move into this area. They had been here longer.

Just gets more and more interesting, she thought.

Two very large wolves walked up to her, golden eyes staring up at her face.

She knew. This was the alpha male and his mate. She guested that the male must weight close to a hundred and fifty pounds while his mate was probably about a hundred and twenty.

This pack, it seemed to her, was spending much more time checking her out, noses making sniffing sound, various of the pack circling around and around her as she stood still and practiced relaxing.

Then, at some silent signal she couldn't see, the pack slipped on silent feet into the forest.

She was alone.

So, once again, she stood and waited.

And waited.

And waited.

The moon had coasted a good distance when she could see shadows approaching, much smaller shadows, slinking through the grass from all sides at once. When they came close enough, she gasped.

At the soft sound everyone of them froze in place, ears up, swiveling, searching for, something.

Coyotes, she said to herself. It is a pack of coyotes. A pack of now nervous animals who smell the scent of wolf in the grass and on her. As they approached, carefully watching her, they, one by one, touched her, cold nose to hand, and slipped away.

The song dogs faded away, disappearing into the woods.

More and more interesting, she thought. If I told anyone about this, they would laugh. Things like that did not happen with wild animals like that, not at all.

She stood and waited.
And waited.
And waited.

And thought about all that had happened. And as she did she realized that the light was changing, the sun was beginning to rise. It was time to go home.

She stretched and yawned, and walked on rather stiff legs back down the game trail. But soon, her legs loosened up and she could lengthen her stride. She was hungry, very hungry.

When she stepped out into the large meadow, she could smell breakfast being cooked.

She increased her pace, and then laughed to herself.

She was feeling as hungry as a wolf.

Not Very Nice

The two brown vans parked side by side in front of *The Stop'n'Go Motel,* one of the two motels on the edge of the small town.

One of the drivers paid for everything, four rooms, double occupancy, for one night. Walking back to the vans he handed out the keys and went to his selected room with the other driver.

The pair spread the topographic map, the Forest Service map, and the aerial photographs on the table and double checked the exact route that they would follow.

They walked from the room, locked one of the vans, and drove off in the other to do a visual check of their chosen route. It would be very late at night when they made the actual drive with everybody aboard and they wanted to be sure that late at night that they wouldn't have to stop and check to see that they were where they wanted to be.

Back at the motel, they rounded up the rest of the crew and drove to the restaurant recommended to them by the motel clerk.

In the restaurant they all ordered the *Specialty of*

The House, very large steaks with heaps of french fries and a large beer. It would be a busy night for them and they all felt the need to eat lots of calories.

Back in the motel, they all set their alarms and went to sleep.

The moon was high overhead when they parked the two vans along the road in the pre-selected spot, facing back in the direction they would go when they were done.

Two remained with the vans to make sure that no one could bother them. This late at night it wasn't very likely, but they were a very careful crew. So two stayed, just in case.

The rest headed along the narrow dirt road toward their target. They didn't hurry, but they walked at a good pace. Their gear and their passage along the road made little noise. They were very good at what they did. Night-time exercises were their specialty.

None of them ever questioned what they were doing or what they were about to do. They were a crew that was handed a bundle of money, told what the goal was, and sent on their way. They went and did it.

They had no need to talk with each other or the pair left behind. Everyone of them knew exactly what they would do, they were a very experienced crew, which was why they were hired.

Surprise late at night worked very well.

On they walked into this tunnel of a road, dense forest bordering either side. The woods absorbed what little noise they made, or anything else that might be moving inside that growth.

Stream's eyes flew open. The moon, high overhead shone bright patches on her bedroom floor.

Then she knew what had wakened her.

She rolled from her bed, quickly yanked on her clothes and boots, and headed down the hall.

Silently she opened the door and slipped inside, and said, "Shhhhhh," as Lou bolted upright.

Amazing, she thought, how he was able to do that.

"We have unpleasant visitors coming up the road."

"What?"

"Shhhhh. Get dressed. Meet me on the porch. Quietly."

She slipped through the living room, eased open the outer door, and stepped outside. The light was bright, the meadow all silver shine.

Sitting on the steps, she fastened up her boots, and peered at where the road entered the meadow. Nothing was moving out there. Yet. But she knew differently.

Lou sat next to her.

"Now what?" he whispered.

"Well, it is basically simple. You find a deep shadow to sit in, and shoot any human other than me that gets within range."

She patted his shoulder.

"And don't worry or try to do anything else, I will be O.K."

He nodded. "O.K. Ummmm?"

"What?"

"Be careful."

"Sure."

She bent sideways and kissed him on the forehead, straightened up, and grinned at his startled expression. She stood and stepped off the porch.

"See ya."

She started out and across the meadow, her dark clothing merging with the forest as she disappeared into it. She was walking on a different game trail than the one she had used earlier.

This one would cross over the road about a third of its length from here.

She strode along, watching the debris. Not stepping on any small branches and other things that would crackle or crack, a dark shadow spirit of the woods.

Ass she walked along she saw them, forest ghosts moving along with her.

Far down the road from where she was, the two empty vans sat there, the ignition keys in the ignition slots, ready to be turned.

Late in the day, two days from now, the Sheriff's officer's vehicles, as they answered the complaint about abandoned vehicles this far out of town, and their boots as they checked the vehicles, would obliterate what little trails they were that might have told what had happened.

Stream slowed up as she could see the slightly lighter patch that was the opening to the road and eased carefully up to and next to a cluster of pine through which she could peer.

As she stood, waiting, coyotes began to yip somewhere on the far side of the road.

The men that she could see stopped, and stared in that direction.

They disappeared as wolves stormed from the forest on either side of the road, bowling the men over as the heavy bodies crashed into them.

All she could see was a mass of milling and bitting wolves. Other than a few startled exclamations, it was a silent struggle.

Quicker than she thought was possible, bodies were being tugged into the woods.

By morning there would be fragments of cloth, boots, and the things that they had been carrying strewn far and wide. In this dense growth, the searchers would be hard pressed to find anything.

Stream sat heavily on the ground and leaned her back against a handy tree trunk, eyes staring into space.

All the feelings of the packs had surged through her mind during that short and brutal struggle. It was not what she had expected. She had felt everything.

Surging to her feet, she began to run, back down the game trail, towards home, towards her mother.

Lou sat in his chosen shadow patch, watching the meadow and the mouth of the road, debating whether he ought to go check on whatever she was up to, or just to stay here until the sun came up. He had heard the coyotes yipping somewhere in the distance over toward the road.

Suddenly a pack of coyotes shot from the forest, turned sharply toward the side of the meadow that was closest to town, and raced that way. They were running as hard as they could and rapidly disappeared.

He had no way of knowing that they were fleeing wolf territory and excited wolves.

Lou stood and stared as the last few shot past, ears laid back, tails streaming straight behind.

The meadow was silent and undisturbed once again.

He slowly walked over and sat on the porch steps, brows slightly furrowed as he wondered what was going on and what was Stream doing out there where something had frightened the coyotes so.

So he sat and waited.

He saw movement. It was Stream hurtling from the forest into the meadow. Her arms and legs were pumping as she raced through the tall grass.

Lou leaped to his feet, eyes scanning the forest edge, searching for whatever she was running from.

As she rushed through the meadow and charged toward him, he could her eyes, wide staring eyes, tears streaming down her cheeks.

Stream shot past him, clearing the steps in a single leap, and shoved into the house, banging the door open back against the wall.

He stared, and turned back, still searching for whatever it was.

Finally, he turned, walked inside, closed the door, and stared.

Stream sat on the couch, a huddled form wrapped in her mother's arms.

Her mother was gently stroking her daughter's hair, making soft soothing sounds. Eventually she was successful. Stream relaxed, sat back and up.

"I felt everything," she gasped. "I felt the excitement of attacking the prey. The anger, if wolves feel anger, at intruders threatening one of their pack. The joy and satisfaction as they ate their fill." She stared at her mother who watched her carefully.

"I was a wolf!" cried Stream.

"Umm ha, not exactly, daughter, not exactly."

"I was one of them. I know that I was."

Her mother nodded slowly.

"But, now you are not."

She handed Stream a fistful of tissues she had just yanked from a box sitting on the couch next to her.

"Dry your eyes, daughter, my not wolf."

Stream did. And slumped, legs sticking straight out.

"It that how it is?"

"Ummm ha, mostly." Her mother nodded. "Now

you listen carefully."

Stream nodded back.

"You have to always know who are, always!"

Stream nodded again.

"What if I forget?"

"That," explained her mother, gently, carefully, "is where all those shape-changer tales come from, from those who forgot who they were."

She stood and tugged her daughter to her feet.

"You need to eat breakfast and then sleep."

She led Stream to the kitchen.

"Come along, Lou, you need breakfast as well."

As they sat at the kitchen table and ate breakfast, Lou looked across the table at the mother. He waited until Stream had headed to her bedroom.

"What was that all about?"

"Fret not, warrior, it was just Stream beginning to understand her heritage as a Special Child."

Lou scooped more onto his plate and waited while she filled his coffee cup.

"Uh huh." He frowned slightly at her.

"Stream is learning special inherited skills. She is just finding out how they work, that is all."

She blew on the coffee she had deliberately poured into her saucer.

"It is always a surprise and it takes some time to be comfortable with it. She will sleep until tomorrow."

She pushed the toaster lever down to start four more slices.

"Last night, eight every bad men were killed and their bodies were eaten by the wolves. During hunting season one or two hunters who are not from around here get lost and their remains never found until years later, if ever."

She began to butter the slices now popped up.

"So and so, one or two lost is a one day, maybe two day, conversation around here, mostly at the town café gathering spot. Eight strangers lost will have tongues waggling for days and days, until something else happens. This may even bring in search parties from outside."

She shrugged.

"Won't find much, if they do find anything. A big mystery. Lots of tongue flutter. Then something else will do for local conversation."

She waggled her hand. "Only four people will really know what happened and they are all in this house."

"Uh huh." Lou was spreading out the strawberry jam on the piece of toast that he held.

"Wakes tomorrow?"

She nodded. "Uh huh, uh huh."

She reached across the table and held his hand, his free hand, the other held the toast he was chewing on.

"You must help her, Lucien. She is a wolf daughter, that is what she is feeling and experiencing. You must be very calm and supportive. There is no one, outside of my husband and I, who could do that."

She handed him another piece of toast and released his hand.

"She was told of a great evil out there. You have seen, with her, its edge. Whatever you two have been doing, this black thing is getting very unhappy about it."

As he started to speak, she held up her hand.

"Tell me not. It is the path that you and my daughter must walk." She smiled at him.

"It is good that you brought sturdy boots and good outdoor wear. She will be wandering all around the forest for the next three or four days. You must be with her, regardless of what she does."

She grinned at him.

"What?" He coated the toast with jam.

"It will be a learning experience for you as well."

With that last statement for him to ponder, she left to wake up her husband.

Dark Questions

Ztrich stood behind his modest desk in his modestly furnished office and leaned on his balled fists as he glared across that desk at his two most senior staff and long-term friends.

James L. took a sip from his coffee cup and nodded.

"It is true, boss."

Z thumped down in his chair and took a large swallow from his coffee cup and pondered whether he ought to pour a little something extra into it.

He grimaced.

"Fergy worked for us for four years?"

"Right," said James L.

"He killed himself way the back and gone from that berg he lived in?"

"Right."

"Right after his body was found every scrap of paper and his computers were taken from his place?"

"Right."

"Not long after that a couple of burglars were killed in this Stream's house?"

"Right."

"She works for some outfit that is so secret and

secure that no one knows anything about them, or will talk about them?"

"Right."

"You sent Samuel and Hank down there to watch her and her assistant, helper, or whatever he is, to see if you could find out anything?"

"Right."

"Those two, against orders, broke into her house and put some sort tracking device on a piece of her camping gear?"

"Right."

"They followed her out into the boonies where she was camping solo and then you told them to eliminate her? Why?"

"Right. Place where she works and the Fergy burglar event seemed too coincidental to me."

"And Hank was killed?"

"Right."

"Local folk keep very close watch on her place?"

"Right. Neighbors."

"An eight man team sent to work over her parents disappeared?"

"Right. Vans were found just sitting by the side of the road, keys in the ignition. Some of their clothes were still at the motel where they stayed. The locals assume that they were just dumb out of the area hunters. It seems a few get lost and disappear there every hunting season, rugged country."

Z sighed, opened a desk drawer, yanked out a

bottle, and removed the cork, and offered it to this associates. He poured some into their held out cups. Then Z did the same to his cup, corked the bottle, left it on the desk top, and toped up the three cups with coffee from the carafe on his desk.

"See the pattern here?"

"Right."

"Tell me."

"Z, this Stream has had almost every record about her eliminated from everything. That takes a lot of skill and power, political pull, to do things like that. Our researchers, mine and Ralph's, spent days and days searching damn near everything in the worlds based just on her first name or ownership of that property she lives in. One of them found a single old newspaper account in an ancient archive of a close to one-man newspaper operation that had a single mention of her. From that they thought that they had located her parents."

"And?"

"As far as is humanly possible it appears that no can find out what, but something with large resources seems to be protecting that young woman. Whoever they are, they are damn lethal. And, as I said, there are no indications of who or what these protectors are. Other than her job, which we could find almost nothing about, there doesn't seem to be anything else that could be responsible."

"O.K. Keep digging. Have we bumped into some

sort of super secret government bunch of spooks?"

Both of the men shrugged.

James L. and Ralph emptied their cups, set them on the desk, and left the office.

Z emptied his cup and treated himself to just a little more from the bottle and then placed it back in its drawer.

He reached over and pulled open another drawer and pulled out a sheet of notes that he had previously made. He hadn't shared these with either James L. and Ralph. He wanted them to work in their own way without any outside bias.

He read his notes again.

Z had reached out and yanked on the strings that he had attached to a sizable number of folk here and there, all of whom had received sizable sums of money for various purposes.

And from them he had gotten, nothing! Of course, all of them were up to their eyes playing politics of one form or another. But one of them had heard the faintest of whispers. He had called Z, on a throw away cell phone, and whispered about that whisper.

He had heard, he said, that various of the legal and law organizations used an outfit that they could hand very difficult problems to understand. Not only that, but that this, probably fictional, place worked on only a few of those difficult problems at a time. That this B-grade movie place did was what the legal and law organizations could not do. They could spent all the time and effort that they wished looking at that problem without outside interference or political meddling.

Z nodded to himself.

He thought that, maybe, they had accidently bumped into this "fictional" outfit.

Now the question was this. What should he do about it?

Just Visiting

Right after breakfast, Stream headed out across the meadow in front of her parent's house. She stopped and looked at Lou.

"You don't have to come along."

He smiled. Her mother had said that she would say that.

"Ummmm."

"What?"

"Yes, I do."

"Do, what?"

"Come with you." He held up one hand. "Ah, ah, no arguing." He laughed. "Mother's orders."

"Oh."

"Yep." He gestured at the game trail opening that he could see just ahead of them. "After you."

It was a nice day to be outside, taking a hike, in and out of the shadow patches inside the forest. Overhead, it was a cloud free day, all blue sky and sunshine.

His pack was stuffed with edibles and water. He figured that it might be a long day.

Following along behind her as she led him along

the game trail toward the small meadow where she had spent a night meeting wolves and coyotes, he admired the view.

My, my, my, he thought, she was truly an attractive person, especially for being a boss in the strange organization for which they both worked. He quickly shoved that thought into some deep recess of his mind. He suspected that following that train of thought could get him in deep trouble, or worse.

Soon they entered a small meadow.

Lou stared at all the flattened grass and wondered what had been going on here.

Stream turned and headed for another game trail that took them steadily uphill. It was an easy but steady grade.

From what little that Lou could see, it appeared to be a rather wide and flat ridge of some type.

Slowly the forest thinned until he could see deeper into the woods on either side of where they were walking. He stared, squinted, and stared again. Large dark shapes, almost visible, most not visible in the dabbled shadows, seemed to be moving parallel to them.

Stream strode along, apparently more focused on where she was heading that anything that might be wandering along with them on either side of the trail.

He followed, wondering where she was headed. And what was going on out there in the forest.

Her father had told him all about her growing up

out here, living surrounded by forest. He told how both parents worried about her excursions that would last all day, but eventually they both realized that she was right at home, totally comfortable, wandering in all that growth by herself and that they should have no worry about her ever getting lost. She seemed to have an internal compass that always guided her back.

Now they stepped out into an open scab patch of ground. Here the ridge was quite steep on one side, fairly gently on the other, leading down intro somewhere not seen.

Lou could see a number of game trails coming up from the steep side and wandering down the gentle side, some followed the ridge. Certainly a popular spot, he thought.

Up ahead of them was a large, open area with a few large boulders sitting here and there.

Stream chose one of them to use as a seat, shrugged off her pack, and began to fish around it. She pulled out something to snack upon.

Lou did the same thing, choosing the closest boulder to hers. He took a small drink of water as well.

Stream looked over. "Just sit quietly and don't make any sudden movements." She looked to her left, back down the way they had come.

He looked the same way, and stopped chewing.

Wolves were walking along the game trail, headed for the same spot where they were sitting.

He sucked in a deep breath, exhaled very slowly,

and sat very still, becoming one with his rock. As least, so he hoped.

The wolves walked at a casual pace, all eyes focused on Stream, apparently ignoring him.

Whatever they were up too, it seemed to him that it was Stream they were focused upon. Not him. Maybe it was because she was a female. Perhaps not. He had not idea what a wolf might think about two humans sitting on rocks in front of the path they were traveling. He sat even more still, if that was possible. It was all that he could do. He certainly couldn't run. He knew dogs could run as fast as twenty miles an hour. He had no idea how fast a wolf could run. Whatever, it meant that no human could outrun one.

He watched as a very large, dark monster walked close to her and sat near her side. The rest of the pack began to sit, some flopped on their sides while some wandered around, never moving too far away.

Lou stared and almost gasped out loud. But he managed to stifle that impulse.

Stream had set her hand on the back of its thick neck and began to lightly stroke the dense fur. She smiled as she did so.

When she stopped, the wolf lay down, giving a loud exhale as it did so. The yellow eyes stared at Lou who almost stopped breathing.

"You are safe," Stream said softly.

So, Lou relaxed, a little, and slowly looked around. It seemed to him that there were wolves everywhere. They kept looking at Stream, then away. Most them seemed to treat him like the rock that he sat upon. As few wandered over to sniff loudly.

Strange, strange, strange, he told himself. This is very strange.

They sat, relaxed, relaxed as the wolves all around them, though Lou, until the wolves apparently decided that it was time to do something else.

The pack walked into the forest.

Stream stood, shrugged on her pack, and said as she pointed, "We're going that way. There is another trail not far along that heads back toward the house and meadow."

Lou nodded, stood, and followed her.

The trail had a branch which curved off and wandered down the slope away from the ridge.

To Lou it appeared that this trail had heavier traffic on it than the one that they had been walking on. Perhaps it was the lure of the large open meadow? He had no idea. But there was where they were headed.

As they walked along, he didn't see any more wild life other than a few deer that they had spooked and a hawk gliding long moments before drifting back up to catch the wind. And little by little he became aware of the silence in the forest. It was a very quiet place. The very denseness of the growth seemed to soak up sound. He realized that he hadn't noticed this earlier but now that he did he began to feel a very pleasant aspect to this kind of solitude of walking in the forest.

He had not realized exactly how noisy most places were with all those cars and trucks driving from here to there, the sound carrying for miles, as did the sound of trains on their tracks and the airplanes overhead, large and small. All in all, the mused, most of the world, at least as it was expressed inside this nation, was littered with sound.

But not out here. It was quiet!

On the way down they passed through several small open areas. In these he saw and heard birds, not a lot, but some, all around the edges. But then he and Stream stepped into quiet again.

Late in the afternoon they strolled into the large meadow not far from the backside of the house. Here her parents had developed a large garden, complete will tall deer fencing to protect the vegetables and fruit trees inside the enclosure.

Stream's mother stood up from whatever she had been doing and smiled at them.

"I made lemonade," she called, "help yourself."

Lou was filling glasses when she entered the kitchen from the back porch, washed her hands in the kitchen sink, and joined them at the table.

"My husband went to town for a few items we needed. He'll be back in time for supper." Her eyes flicked from face to face.

"Have a good hike?"

"Yep," replied Lou. "Very pleasant."

"Yep," agreed Stream. "Very pleasant."

Her mother nodded, and smiled at them.

Then they sat on the front porch and talked quietly about the weather and other inconsequential things until Stream and her mother headed back inside to start cooking supper.

Not long after, a truck rattled from the forest on the dirt road, drove up and parked by the side of the house.

Her father climbed out, took a large bag from the rear seat, and headed inside. "Heya, Lou."

He returned, holding two bottles of beer, already opened, and handed one to Lou.

"Made locally," he said. "Dark beer. Hope you like it."

Lou took a swallow. "Really good."

"I think so. Have a good day?"

"Uh huh. Got lots of exercise. Feels good to just sit and relax."

"She did that from a very early age, walking the game trails, exploring all around the place. She eventually knew a patch that stretched a few miles in every direction. She knew that piece of ground better than anyone around here. She even found a lost hunter, now and then." He laughed.

"Those guys were really surprised when a young girl strolled from somewhere and told them to follow her and that she would see to it that they returned to where they parked their rig."

Lou nodded and added, "I am not surprised."

And he wasn't, not for the next three days as he followed Stream as she coursed through the forest, slowly revisiting everything on all sides of the meadow as well as some of the denizens that lived out there.

He got to sit a lot and watch wolves visit with her.

He found that he was not only getting used to that but he caught himself forgetting that these great canines were carnivores at the top of the food chain and not just large and friendly dogs.

Unlike Stream, he never reached out to touch one, although he felt himself about to do that. Then he reminded himself, these were wild animals, wolves with very large teeth, and that he really needed all his fingers.

They spend a few days just lounging and taking naps, until Stream announced, "It is time to go back to work. Can't have the boss chewing his nails to the quick wondering where we are."

In the early dawn, they packed everything in her truck, got hugged by both parents, and started back.

They followed a different set of two lane roads as much as possible, camping here and there. One day's travel from home, Stream changed her license plates back to the originals.

Mystery

Ztrich swivelled from looking out his modest office window at the blue sky dotted with white puffy clouds and looked at this number one staff and long time friend who had just walked into the office unannounced.

Z raised his eyebrows and filled an empty coffee cup with coffee, handed it over, and nodded.

James L. took the cup, sat, took a sip, and cleared his throat.

"Things are just not making a whole lot of sense out there, Z."

"About?"

"Complicated story."

Z nodded.

"You know the high paid researchers we paid tons of money to are the ones that found that single newspaper article that mentioned that girl, Stream?"

Z nodded again, and took a sip.

"We assumed that the couple living in the back country acreage inside the forest were her parents and that the girl was their daughter, Stream Sidling."

Z took sip.

"No birth record of such a person."

James L. held up his hand.

"All that money that we spent finally found out who owns the house where this Stream babe lives."

Z smiled at him.

"The kicker is that the property is owned by a person named Janae Dawn."

Z sat back and took another sip, brows slightly furrowed.

"We have a person inside the I.R.S., who just got fired, who found something that he shouldn't have been poking his nose into. It looks like he will spent a few years in a federal lockup. But!"

James L. took a sip from his coffee cup and held it out. Z refilled it.

"He gave us a copy on the report for taxes paid by Janae Dawn before one of his co-workers realized he was prowling around where he shouldn't be prowling. Hence the arrest, etc."

Z sighed.

James L. nodded.

"Janae Dawn, known, on one of the reservations, as She-Who-Watches-The-Sun-Rise, is Stream. It seems that a few years back there was some problem about that property that caused the owner to come in and pay some kind of fee. The researcher flashed the clerk, who seems to be a permanent fixture there, a photograph, and the clerks says, yep, that is the owner of the property, always pays everything on time, other than that one-time mix up."

Z sat up and stared at him.

"The tax stuff shows that Dawn gets a large monthly salary and pays all the usual things, and listed social security number, etc."

"So," said Z, "this Stream name is an alias?"

"Certainly looks like it."

"We were going after the wrong folk?"

James L. nodded. "That too."

"What?"

"Well, the Stream persona does get to spend a whole lot of time wandering around out in the boonies by herself. This is what our watchers could find out and see for themselves."

Z exhaled loudly.

"So we have pissed off some southwestern tribe?"

James L. shrugged.

"That could explain our guys being dead and missing."

"Crap!"

"Yes."

"So, who are her parents, then?"

"No idea. The reservations records are lots of very bad book keeping, depending upon which one, depending on how far back you try to go."

"She doesn't look like an Indian."

"Lots of intermarriage going on from the time people migrated from the east coast into all that western territory."

Z refilled their cups.

"What else do we know?"

"Little. Found a driver's license for Janae Dawn, a picture license. Same face."

"Still watching her place of employment and her residence?"

"Problem there."

"What?"

"Nervous neighbors don't like strangers. People have gotten sent to the hospital. Rough neighborhood. Three folk watching her work place have disappeared."

"And we really do not know anything, do we?"

"Other than two different names, not much."

"A mystery."

"Yes, it is."

My, My, My

Stream dropped Lou off at his place and as soon as he removed his stuff from the back of her truck, headed for her home.

In front, she parked, unlocked the entry gate, shoved it open, drove the truck to its parking spot, and spotted the lights that were on in the kitchen.

She shoved the front door open and strode for the kitchen. She could smell something cooking, loading the air with all those tasty smelling spices.

"Welcome, home."

Stream smiled at her.

"Thanks, Lupe. Who's cooking?"

"Grandmother sent it over. It just got to the point where it is ready to eat." She waggled one hand at the two place settings on the kitchen table.

"Where's your partner?"

"His place. We had a long drive. Join me?"

Lupe grinned. "Love to." She turned the stove off, collected the two plates and heaped them full.

"Lots of chilies and other good things."

"Smelled like it. How did you know?"

"Didn't." Lupe shrugged. "Grandmother started

the dish this morning and told me when to come over with it."

Stream shrugged and shook her head.

"Never fails to amaze me."

Lupe laughed.

As they ate, Lupe explained how everyone in the neighborhood was watching her place and what had happened to those "strangers" that had come around, poking and prying, and asking questions.

"Some folk got a little rough with them," she said.

Then she shrugged. "But no-one has heard a word from the cop shop about it."

Stream nodded. "Ah, well." She stood and refilled her plate and looked the question at Lupe.

"I'm fine. Good trip?"

"Yep. Had a good time. We camped here and there and then wandered the forest around my parent's place."

Lupe stood.

"I will tell Grandmother. And leave you with the dirty dishes."

She stood, headed for the front door, calling over her shoulder, "I'll lock the gate."

"See ya," called Stream. Then she piled the dishes in the sink, ran hot water over them as she added the soap. The cooking pot and its leftover contents would have to cool before she could attend to that.

She headed down the hall, took a long, hot bath,

and headed to bed.

Bright and early, she banged into her office, started the coffee maker there, checked whatever had crawled into her In-Box, and smiled as he wandered in.

"I really slept," Lou announced, taking a cup and heading over to fill it as the system made loud gurgling sounds that announced that it was finishing.

He turned and stared at her desk top and the litter. "So, what's new?"

"Boss wants us in Meeting Room A in half an hour. Other than that, not much."

"He mad at us?"

"Never!"

"Ummmm?"

"Don't really know, but it is very unusual."

"Ah?"

"Wait and see, wait and see." She stood and filled her cup.

"Any idea?"

"Nope."

By the time they had emptied their coffee cups and did what little paperwork there was to do, it was time to go.

"This way," she said, leading him in the right direction.

He nodded.

Meeting Room A was a small room, furnished with over-stuffed chairs. It was to be used for small groups, four to six, to meet in a comfortable setting.

Meeting Room B had a much more corporate look to it. Large, long table, lots of chairs on all sides.

The boss looked at them as they entered, large cigar stuffed in one corner of his mouth. He sat in the chair directly under the ceiling vent. Cigar smoke rose straight up and disappeared into somewhere.

"Hi, boss," she said and sat in the chair that was, more or less, facing him.

Lou sat in a chair, set at a slight angle. He could watch both of them.

Stream waited.

The boss looked from Stream to Lou and back again.

"Your neighbors beat up a number of guys that they thought were trying to pry into your business."

"I heard," she said.

"The Shadow Crew picked up three guys trying to watch this place."

"That I didn't hear."

"We, ah, did a deep check on those three, and the others." He puffed smoke at the ceiling vent.

"And?" she urged.

"From conversations with them, and this and that, it appears that they, and their behavior, all link to the Fergy data. We'll discuss that later."

He stood and handed her two sheets of paper.

"All your's. Room 1, Room2. Take all the time that you wish."

She read them.

"My, my, my."

"Certainly is." The boss stood and headed for the door, trailing smoke. "Tell me anything that I need to know."

He held the door open for them, then headed down the hall toward his office. Stream and Lou headed in the other direction.

"Not good, partner, not good at all."

"What?"

"Whenever he smokes one of those monsters, he is very bothered. A rare event. Let's have a talk."

She pushed open the door to Room 1, and stepped in, Lou right behind her.

A man sat at the small table. He looked up at them.

"I demand an explanation, young lady!"

Lou judged him to be in his high fifties, low sixties, dressed in a very expensive suit, with matching everything else. A rather moneyed individual.

"Stop the histrionics!" snapped Stream as she sat facing him.

His eyes popped wide, but he did. Then he stared, hard, at her. "You!" he gasped.

She ignored him, read one of the sheets of paper that she was holding, set them on the table, face down, and said, "My name is Stream. My partner's name is Lou. You have been a very bad boy, Dr. Harris."

He cleared his throat.

"Exactly what are you talking about, implying?"

She smiled at him. Not what he was expecting.

"It seems, Doctor Harris, that you have been busy, busy, busy, trying to find out about me. You did find a very old newspaper article that mentioned my name. This led you to my parents and where they lived."

"Nothing wrong with that!" he snapped.

"Well, Doc, it seems that you provided information to some people who sent some people, based upon that information, to do bad things to my parents. That makes you, in my mind, an accessory to their intended mayhem, illegal behavior. You could spent a long time teaching ugly fellows how to read and write."

Harris swallowed loudly, his face turning red.

"Sounds pretty bad, huh?" said Stream.

He slowly nodded. "I had no idea of what use they would make of what I found."

"Well, Doc, ignorance is not a very good defense. So, tell me, do you have the name of the persons, or persons, who hired you?"

He reached into a inside pocket of his jacket and slid out a small leather covered case. Opening it, he extracted a card with writing on it, and handed it to her.

Lou eased his hand out of the side jacket pocket as he released his grip on his gun.

"Here! This is the name that I was given and the mailing address where I was to sent whatever I could find."

"Thank you. Didn't you ever think about the large amount of money that someone was willing to pay you to do your work?"

He nodded. "I did, a little. But I expect to be paid well. The project seemed perfectly innocent to me. I was told that you were a reclusive celebrity of some sort and that this person wanting the data was writing a biography of, eh, you."

"So, you were totally focused on me and not, say, real estate and things like that?"

He nodded. "Yes. There was so little that I could find that I was surprised. I am very good at what I do. To find so little made we think that it might be some sort of elaborate piece of writing masquerading as a biography of some sort."

"So, what did you find?"

"Just a first name in one old newspaper archive, a single article, and your family name, which was mentioned. I tried to trace your parents backgrounds which led me into many blind alleys. I found that your father's father was from one of the northern European countries but that the spelling of the family had been changed so heavily that looking further didn't work. I could find nothing on your mother's name so that led nowhere as well. There doesn't seem to be a birth record that I could find. In my terms, you are a ghost, a body with almost no substance at all."

She smiled at him. "Interesting concept. So, you gonna retire to tropical island somewhere. You actually could, given what you were paid, and how much you have stashed in accounts here and there."

He sucked in his breath, his face turning red again.

"We are also good at what we do, Doc. Have you told me all you know about your employer on this project of your's?"

"Yes. A name, a way to send him what I found. He put the money into my account, bank transfer of some kind." He shrugged.

"Thanks." Stream stood, stepped over to the door and pushed one of the many buttons.

In a moment the door opened and a stocky man looked in.

"Dr. Harris, this is Francisco. He will escort you. My boss would like to speak with you." They all stepped into the hall. Stream watched that pair walk away and around a corner.

"So far, so good. Let's go see the other guy."

She opened the door across the hall from where they stood. The label on the door stated: Room 2.

This room was identical to Room 1 but the person sitting and waiting wasn't anything like Dr. Harris.

He was a very large man, large not fat. He was dressed in what appeared to be clothes that had seen better days.

Stream sat across from him while Lou selected a chair were he could watch both of them, especially this guy. His hand grasped the gun in his pocket.

Stream read the second piece of paper and set it face down on the table.

"Is Periscope really your name?"

His voice was a harsh gravel that seemed to rumble up from somewhere deep in his chest.

He smiled at her, cheeks heavily dimpled.

"For many, many moons and a lot longer than that, it has been."

She nodded.

"A work name?"

The smile grew even broader. "It is what I do."

"Hunt silently, no one sees you?"

"Precisely."

"We found you."

"Which I find interesting, maybe even fascinating, perhaps amazing as well."

"You were searching for information dealing with real estate, were you not?"

He nodded, eyes watching her face intently.

"And?"

"It was, how to put it, unusual, a kind of subtle unusual."

"Ummmm. We would like to know who paid you, and where and how they received their information from you."

"Not what I found?"

Stream smiled at him.

"Ahhhhh, I see."

She nodded. "I do hope so."

"May I bargain?"

"Perhaps. So, tell me."

"Paper and pen, please."

"Pull out the drawer. Take what you need."

He did. And quickly wrote a number of sentences in a flowing script and shoved the sheet across the table top to her.

"This is all that I know. That name hired me and that address if where I mailed all that I found, not much. I wrote it all out and sent it in."

She smiled at him and tapped one fingertip on the paper

"You must have practiced a long time."

He nodded.

"What did you find, in general."

"Ownership tracking backward in time to some of the earliest settlement of the town, being held always by the same family. Not much else. Reservation records are few and far between for most of their history with outsiders."

He shrugged.

"Driver's license and owner's name indicate that you are a very hard to find anything out about someone named Janae Dawn, or, She-Who-Watches-The-Sun-Rise."

He held his arms out to the side.

"And that is about it. Vague background. No school, etc. records with either name, and on and on and on and on. Very pale-skinned, even for one of your lineage, has to be due to Europeans somewhere in there somewhere."

He grunted.

"It was good and plentiful money for finding out so little. But the buyer didn't seem concerned with the cost. Some sort of eccentric, I suppose. See that every once in awhile." He shrugged. "Just part of the business that I do."

Stream set the sheet he had written upon with the others, stood, walked over to the door, and pushed one of the buttons.

In a moment, the door opened.

Something that looked like a pro-football offensive lineman looked in.

"This is Sammy. This is Periscope. Mr. P, Sammy will guide you. My boss wishes to speak to you."

She walked Lou back to their office.

Once inside, she pulled up her phone, punched a button, and said when someone answered, "Names, mailing addresses, bank accounts, etc." And hung up.

She opened a large envelope, slid all the sheets into it, and handed it to the young man as he walked in.

"Have fun," she said as he took the envelope and hurried away.

"Perhaps," she said to Lou, "we will find out what is all behind this."

Now What?

It had been a rather quiet two weeks as their business went about its business.

Ztrich looked across his modest desk in his modest office and filled the three cups with coffee, handing one to each of his two most senior staff and long-time friends.

He took his cup, sat, and leaned back in his chair, and took a sip. Then he nodded at them.

James L. looked at Ralph and then back at Z.

"Z," he said, " you know we each, Ralph and I, hired the best researcher than we could find."

Z nodded.

James L. sucked in a deep breath.

"It has been a couple of weeks since either of us has heard from them, so we sent some folk to visit them in their homes just to ask how things were going. They usually send us us stuff more frequently, so we thought to just, ahhh, visit."

Z took another sip and then refilled all the cups.

James L. looked at Ralph, who cleared his throat.

"The guy that I hired," stated Ralph, "called himself Periscope. We did a big background check on him because he was a little," he waggled one hand, "peculiar."

Z raised one eyebrow.

"This guy never earned anything else than the grade of A through high school. After he graduated he enrolled in a number of different collages and universities. He had no problem getting in to anything that he applied to. In those places he took whatever courses that interested him, getting nothing but As. Finally in this big time university, the psychology types convinced him to let them give him a series of tests. What happened was not what those researchers thought. He blew through every test that they gave him, including all the egg head mensa super brain things. He blew through them as fast as he could read them. They gave up. What they found out, so to speak, was that this guy was someone that they couldn't measure, other than, as far as they could figure, is that he is some sort of super genius."

Ralph took a swallow from his coffee cup.

"After all that, he dropped out, and legally changed his name to Periscope. Then he opened his research business, charging high fees, and doing those jobs that he felt like doing. He made, makes, very big, big bucks."

Ralph held out his cup, Z filled it.

"Here's the kicker." Ralph took a sip from his cup.

"Periscope lives in a rat-hole basement in a rat-hole building in a rat-hole part of town that even cops avoid. He buys all his clothes at second hand stores and places like that. He is known to sit on the curb and spend time talking with some rat-hole resident that lives in that rat-hole area, drinking rot gut wine from a brown paper bag."

He paused.

"I sent two of our biggest, meanest to visit his dump. Only it wasn't. His basement was, ahhh, comfortable, furnished with second hand furniture and other stuff. He had installed heavy metal doors, both on the outside entrance to his place, and in the hole through the basement wall into the next basement. All the basements walls have big holes in them. The residents can go from place to place and never be seen. Periscope's place was empty of all paper and the hard drives were missing from all his computing gear, and he had lots of those."

Ralph leaned back in his chair and took a sip.

"There is no way to know where he went. If you can find someone to talk to, that is, which you mostly can't."

James L. nodded.

"My turn."

He took a sip and held out his cup, Z filled it.

"My guy is a Mister Clean, professor type with a number of degrees. He opened his research endeavors a number of years back. He is considered to be one of the best. He lives well, dresses well, eats well, etc., etc."

He nodded at Z.

"There was no sign of life in his house. Nicely furnished, good art on the walls, fancy kitchen. But! No paper, and his computing gear is also missing the hard drives."

He laughed.

"In the fancy neighborhood were he lives, lived, no-one can really see much of their neighbors. Lots of trees, lots of space. Best guess is that about a week ago is when he went missing. At least, that was the last time anyone remembered seeing him."

Z sat up, set his cup on the table.

"Both researchers and all their stuff? Gone?"

Ralph nodded.

So did James L.

"Sounds an awful like that Fergy thing. Think that they are dead?"

"No idea, Z," replied James L.

"Doesn't seem likely given who they are," added Ralph.

Z sighed.

"Do either of you think that this Stream broad is somehow connected with any of this?"

"Doubt it," said James L.

Ralph nodded his agreement.

"O.K. We got everything that they could find anyway. Right?"

"Sure," said James L.

Ralph nodded.

They both stood and left the office.

Z swivelled around and watched some low hanging clouds drifting to the east. Then he began to ponder what sort of action ought to be used to bring his message clearly across. He felt that somehow she was responsible for all this.

Culture Clash

Two weeks had past in rather quiet work.

Stream and Lou had put together two reports, final reports, for two rather small projects.

They found that they worked together very well in those endeavors.

Stream was very good at straightening out convoluted sentences and simplifying the language used.

Lou was equally good at maintaining the logic of the presentation and making sure that every and all conclusions were derived directly from the factual data discussion in the body of the work. In addition, he had convinced Stream to make every report at least one of two volumes. The first small volume was the bare facts of the report and the conclusions. The second, and often much larger, volume contained all the supporting documentation in all its original formats. He argued that those receiving these reports would read the first volume and, only as necessary, the second or third volumes of supporting matter.

They had received compliments on this new format from those receiving the reports.

Over coffee early in the third week, she had told him that the results of what all were now calling The Fergy Project, being all the original Fergy materials augmented by file cabinets of additional paper from each of the groups that had been raided so swiftly that they hadn't had time to destroy anything.

All in all, the results of the several reports had helped legal and law forces to pretty much clean up the state as far as that organization went.

The actions taken so far where beginning to spread to adjoining states in a kind of bandwagon effect. From all that, the folk were learning, it appeared that this organization was wide spread, well organized, and had been in existence for many years. Not only that, this outfit had learned how to be invisible in spite of all the illegal activities that they were involved with.

Tuesday had started normally.

Stream opened an envelope from her in-box, pulled out and read the sheets, and snarled.

Lou snapped upright from what he had been doing over by the computers and stared at her.

"WHAT?"

"That group is beginning to irritate me."

Lou sighed.

"What group? What now?"

She stood, walked over to the coffee machine, poured a cup full, and walked back to sit in the chair next to him.

"I think that it is the same bunch, some of whom

recently disappeared in the forest near my folk's place."

"Ummmmm?"

She waggled the papers at him.

"My parents were in town running some small errands. They were standing in front of a store looking in the window at a large display of gardening tools when this guy stepped up behind them. He whispered to them that wise parents would convince their only daughter that it would be in everyone's best interest that she change jobs, find something else to do. And if she didn't do that, well, accidents do happen."

"Ahhh."

"Then he made a mistake."

"Such as?"

"He grabbed my mother's arm."

Lou shrugged.

"Lou, my father is a very, very calm person. He is one of those persons that remains calm in the middle of the worse disaster you can imagine, and see what needs to be done. Not one of those weeping and running about, doing nothing types."

"Uh huh."

"However, he does react quickly, if he has to. He broke that guy's arm and tossed him through the plate glass window. A Sheriff's Deputy was standing not too far away and saw it, and heard it, happen."

"Umm."

"As far as they, County and town cops, can find out, it seems that this guy is linked to the missing so-called hunters."

She emptied her cup, stood, and walked over to refill it. She turned and sighed heavily.

"Eh?"

"I think that The Fergy Project has turned over a very large rock and the very large snakes are getting very nervous and are thrashing around."

He nodded.

"I suppose. Any ideas?"

"One."

"Which is?"

"A writer of science fiction, Iain M. Banks, coined the term in one of the books that he wrote, *out of context problem*. He saw it as a term about cultural clash, when one culture bangs into another and finds that they have a problem that they have never seen before, nor have the experience, cultural knowledge, of what to do about it. That is the problem that they face, an out of context to their culture problem."

"Uh huh."

"I think that I am their out of context problem. Their reactions so far have been standard, classic U.S.A. thug, large organization thug. What The Fergy Project has done is begin to wreck some part of a very large organization, a very large thug organization. I do not, we do not, react the way their culture expects folk to react when they bring to bear their normal, for them, thug approach to solving a problem. Their world view, their culture does not have a mind set for it, thus, the out of context problem. For them."

"O.K." He walked over and refilled his cup. "So, what do we do about that?"

She shrugged. "No idea. Yet." She laughed.

"What?"

"Any stranger that happens to visit is going to have dozens of eyes watching them. Here and around where my parents live."

She set her cup in the sink and walked over to the outside door to her office. "So, O.K., I have an idea."

She opened the door.

"See ya in the morning, Lou. I am going to visit this anthropologist that I know and discuss this with him. After all, culture and cultural behavior is something that they understand."

She started down the hall to the outside.

Final Decision

Ztrich watched as his two most senior staff and log-time friends walked into his modest office and sat in their usual chairs. Each set a small suitcase next to their chair.

"Z," said James L., "I remember when we three started planning our operation, our organization, in high school. We studied everything we could find about how other large operations were found, got busted, and their folk sent to jail."

Z smiled at that memory.

"I remember." He nodded at them. "It took us those three years to get it all together. Our folks thought that we were playing some sort of board game like all the other high school kids were playing."

Ralph smiled. "And it worked out pretty much like we had planned. We found all the things that attracted attention from the law dogs and got rid of them. No big spending, nothing beyond reported income capable, no drug dealing of any kind."

Z smiled back at him and refilled the three coffee cups.

As they all sipped, he asked, "Suitcases? Is it

time?"

"Yep," said James L. "We planned for it, and it has arrived."

Ralph took a sip. "We made a fatal mistake with Fergy."

Z nodded.

"We all agreed to do it," stated James L. "However, as good as it looked, here we are. Unintended consequences."

Z stood, walked around his desk and shook each of their right hands, holding them in a firm grip for a long time.

He smiled at them as he sat on the front edge of his desk.

"We had a good run. Everyone who had kids got them through college. None of them were allowed inside the organization."

Now his smile shifted, it was a very sad smile. "We did plan for this, even if we hoped that it wouldn't happen."

His eyes wandered around his office. "I really am going to miss this place."

He nodded.

"O.K., go send the termination notice. And hope that as many as possible will be able to slip away and into their carefully crafted, anonymous lives."

He stood.

"I'll see you guys in a few weeks or so. Hurry it up. No wasted time. No stalling. Go do it, then get out of this building. I will leave here in just a few minutes, but I do have just a few small things to attend to. And then, I am out of here forever and out of sight."

He shook their hands, one more time, and everybody patted everyone on the back in very tight bear hugs.

As Z watched the pair walk out of his office for the last time, he said "Hurry!"

Then he sat at his desk, swivelled around for a last look out his window, dragging his telephone with him. He punched a button, telling the person who answered, "Release them," and hung up.

It was his last decision. But he felt that it needed to be done.

Turning back to his desk, he stood, picked up his coffee cup, and left his office, headed down the hall and outside to take a slow stroll and ponder what he thought they would do next.

The three of them would have all the time they needed, to sit, to argue, and to plan.

Acts Of War

Stream and Lou were casually strolling down a side street headed back to work after lunch. It had been a quiet number of days, discounting all the paperwork that they had to do.

It had been one more place that Stream had taken him to. Another one that Lou hadn't seen before. He was amazed at how many they were in this area. This one had been all 1920s decor and lighting. But the food had been well-prepared and very good. So, they had a leisurely lunch.

Now, satiated with good food, feeling pleasantly relaxed, they strolled toward work. They turned the corner just two blocks from their office. And stopped. And stared.

Right in front of their building there were lots of flashing lights, fire engines, police cars, and ambulances.

They didn't run to see what was going on, but they did hurry.

Then they stopped across the street from work, standing with the onlookers, and stared again.

The bullet proof glass outer wall and entry door

were mostly gone. Glass shards were strewn from the top of the concrete stairs to the middle of the street.

Lou pointed at the stone wall on either side of the entryway. "Pocks marks, fresh."

Stream was focused on the gore she could see on those concrete stairs and watched the three ambulances leave the scene.

"What the," she said.

"Hell!" finished Lou.

A large man in a crisp uniform walked over to them.

"Howdy, Sheriff," said Lou.

"Big John," greeted Stream. "What happened here?"

"Still working on that, Stream. We got called out, shots fired, bodies lying about."

"That's it?"

Big John shrugged. "So far. Quite a mess."

He waggled at hand at the numbers of uniformed personnel doing things, here and there.

"Wait here, they're almost done."

Stream sighed, crossed her arms over her chest, and waited.

Lou stood silently next to her.

A very nondescript man walked from the crowd of bystanders and stopped just behind them.

"Four guys jumped out of that black van you see over there. The two in front ran at the entryway firing heavy weapons that eventually shattered it. Two others were right behind them, cradling automatic weapons with very long banana clips. Three dead, one punctured a few times. That one ought to live and answer our questions."

He turned away and faded back into the crowd.

Lou nudged her.

"What?"

"Who was that?"

"Shadow Crew."

"Oh."

Big John waved them over.

"We're done. Watch the glass. I'll let you know if we find out anything about what happened here."

As soon as the streets were empty of police cars and fire department rigs, a large van pulled up, followed by another.

Men wearing working clothes and coveralls began to remove the debris and dismantle the remains of the entry wall.

"That was fast," observed Lou.

"Yep. Shall we go in? Go back to work?"

"Sure."

They carefully walked up the stairs and down the hallway to her office. And went back to work.

They were thirty minutes into a new report, the other one sat on her desk, nice cover and all, when Rala burst into the office.

"I have it!" she announced.

Lou looked over at her smiling face. She was

holding a large, thick sandwich in one hand.

"Ham on rye?" he asked.

Stream waited, stifling her smile.

"No!' Rala shook her head. "It is pumpernickel, Swiss cheese, and pepperoni, butter on one slice, horseradish spread on the other."

Stream winked at Lou. "Have some coffee, Rala."

"Thanks." Rala carefully set her sandwich on Stream's desk, on top of the just finished report, and hurried over to the coffee maker.

Stream watched horseradish sauce slowly ooze from the sandwich onto that new cover. She shrugged.

"You always have such good coffee, Stream. And fair traded, too!"

"Rala?"

She turned, took a sip, and nodded.

"Really good."

"What did you mean when you said, I have it?"

"Oh." She set her cup next to the sandwich, adding a coffee ring to the sauce stain.

From one pocket of her baggy sweater she yanked out a rumpled, folded piece of paper. She opened it and spread it over Stream's desk, pens and pencils. It was a map of the western states heavily decorated with wildly drawn red circles.

Stream looked at it. "Measles."

"Oh, no," gasped Rala. "I feel fine."

"All those circles."

"I drew them. It is a glowing red marker I bought

in that super inexpensive shop down the block."

"What are they?"

"I did that. From all the reports. You know, the stuff all the agencies send us."

"And?"

"These are all the places that they have raided, so far, from information from The Fergy Project. It is all over the place, a really large organization."

"Wow," said Lou.

"Oh, yes," agreed Rala.

"This is what you wanted to show us?" asked Stream.

Rala folded the map into a compact mess and stuffed it back into her pocket. From the other pocket she extract a somewhat crumpled single sheet of paper.

"No. This is it! I found the names of the bosses, sorta."

"Sorta?"

Rala nodded vigorously.

"Yes. They hardly ever get mentioned by name in all that paper. But I found three names, here and there."

"And they are?"

"Ztrich, James L., and Ralph. From what I read, these three tell everyone else what to do."

Stream held out her hand. Rala gave her the paper.

"The researchers," stated Rala, "got really excited. Especially about the Z name. Something that unusual they thought would make it easier for them to find."

Rala picked up her sandwich and cup of coffee and headed for the door to the office.

"Thanks for the coffee. Who made such a mess in the hall?"

She headed back toward her office.

"Holy cow!" Lou watched Rala walking away, down the hall. "How can see not be aware of that mess?"

"Hyper-insulated, sound proof rooms for her to work in, remember."

Lou nodded and smiled.

"Looks like," said Stream, examining the map again, "that we really banged into something that we didn't expect."

"From the number of circles, I'd say so."

Her phone rang. She picked it up. Yes?" And listened. And hung up.

Lou stared at her. Her expression had something in it that he hadn't seen before. It wasn't good.

"Stream?"

"Somebody tried to blow up my house. They got as far as turning the gate into kindling.

Lou thudded down into his seat.

"What is going on?"

"I am," she growled, "going to do very bad things to some bad people!"

Where The Call Leads

Stream parked her large pickup at the end of a marginal four-wheel jeep road, and jumped down, and took a deep breath of high mountain air.

"Well," she said as Lou walked around the truck to stand near her. "Here we are." He looked around.

She pointed. "That is wilderness. Nothing but trails, no roads. No motorized anything allowed. So, in there, there are people hiking, horse and mule riding. Folk leading llamas. The route we are taking means that we probably won't see anyone, which is good."

Stream laughed.

"That means we can see anyone trying to follow us."

They walked to the rear of the truck, opened the back end, and began to pull out their already assembled back packs and set them on the beginnings of the trail that they would follow.

"There is no hurry. We'll take it slow. We have more than enough supplies to give us days and days. It's primitive camping all the way. Ready for that?"

"Sure." Lou picked up his gear, swung it into place, and made a few minor adjustments.

He winked at her. "Ready when you are, Gridley."

Stream pushed her pack up and down, a little, and winked back. She locked the truck.

"I'll tell you what we are up to at our first camp. Here we go." She headed down the trail. "We will go rather slow. It will take a few days for us to acclimate."

Stream was carrying the necessary detailed maps, especially made for this trip.

They made camp in mid-afternoon. It would take a few days of hiking to acclimate them to this area.

"Like I said." Stream dropped her back pack next to herself. She pointed. "We can sleep right there, just far enough off the trail for safety. Don't want some horse string trying to get to someplace in the dark and stepping on us."

They cooked, in a manner of speaking, their meal on tiny stoves, and ate the results.

Stream propped her pack against a tree trunk and sat on the pine duff using the pack as a back rest.

"Researchers found the names of the trio that controlled everything and made all the decisions. They are Ztrich Ziminsky, James Laparona, and Ralph Anders, all chums since grade school. I have a map that show exactly where they are now living. Three separate places. We are going to visit them and reply to all the favors they gave so willingly to others."

Lou sprawled on his sleeping gear, on his side.

"O.K., sounds good to me."

"Lou, what I am planning isn't going to be even close to being anything legal. You could just camp a day out from their places, claim total ignorance of whatever happens."

"Nope!" He smiled a lopsided smile at her. "I figure you have some idea of how we are going to avoiding getting into that kind of trouble." Then he added, "I hope."

"Yep, certainly do. But it won't be nice." She frowned at something.

"O.K. I brought a bag of cookies. Want some?" He held it out to her. "Take two, they're small." And laughed.

In the morning they were up almost as early as the sun.

As soon as they had eaten breakfast, Stream consulted her map and off they went, stopping for lunch in whatever spot looked good to them, often selected for the scenic view. There were many opportunities to chose from.

As daylight began to fade, they selected their camping spot, made dinner, and took to their sleeping bags.

This routine was regulated by the terrain they were hiking in and the daylight hours, much like the other day dwelling animals here abouts.

Often the trail they followed was little more than a goat track, so narrow that they had to walk single file, the deeply worn trail barely wider than their boots.

And so it went, day after day after day.

And they found that they were beginning to hike easier, breath easier, their steps were more limber.

Now, they often talked as they walked, about nothing in particular, often about the scenery.

Late in the afternoon, Stream halted them, and selected their camp spot.

As they settled in, and after they ate, she said, "Now I am going to tell you something that happened to me that you may not want to believe, but, none the less, is absolutely true. It is why we are here, much more than merely to rid the world of some folk who wanted to kill us."

Lou chewed on a cookie and shoved the almost empty bag toward her, rather puzzled, and watched her take two of the remaining cookies.

"O.K.," he said. "Tell me." He sat cross-legged, elbows on knees and watched her face.

She did and took a bite from one of the cookies.

She told him of camping in that ancient dwelling spot, one that she had visited many times before, mainly because of its isolation. She spoke of her nocturnal visitors and what they had told her. When she finished she looked at him, face carefully blank. "And you heard my mother call me a Special Child. I'll tell you all about that, ummmm, later." She sighed and wondered how her life got to this state of affairs other than the obvious problems. Of course, her mother had said she had to recognize what she was and to not fuss about it.

"O.K." Lou nodded at her.

"That's it? O.K.?"

"Yep."

"When we get back, I'll take you there and you can see the place for yourself."

"Sure." He thought that visiting that place could be very interesting.

Stream bent over one of the maps and then explained how they would proceed from here.

They would stash their gear at the spot that looked good to her and put a notice that would be visible to anyone that might stumble on their stuff, saying that they would return in one day. If that happened, most hikers would leave everything alone. If not, they would figure out what to do after that.

She flattened out that map and pointed.

"In that direction are their houses. They are not too close to each other but not very far apart either. We will follow this jeep trail. It is just outside the wilderness boundary and runs parallel to it. A third of a day, half at the worst to the first place, then we move to the next and the next. And return to here. A rather long day, but doable."

Lou nodded.

"Tomorrow we lay about and rest. As early as possible the day after that we are on the move carrying light, only what we absolutely require to do what I believe is necessary."

Lou looked at her. "And then?"

"A casual hike across the wilderness and back to home."

"O.K." He stretched out on his sleeping gear.

The next day they did rest and lounge about and eat three large meals.

Before the sun peeked above the horizon, in the dim twilight, they were on their way, hiking on the jeep trail.

She told him that there were numerous offshoots along this jeep trail and that there were no sign posts.

"Lots of crappy roads. Hard to get here."

"Yep." Stream consulted her map. "Those three hoods like privacy. All the worse for them. Here we go."

She headed them down one of the branches that broke away from the main trail.

"Not far ahead we should see a log building in a large clearing."

She pointed at a spot ahead where the light was brighter. "You can tell by the light that we are almost there."

She picked up the pace.

"Ready, partner?"

"Yep."

They stopped just inside the forest, in the shadows and peered out.

It was a large structure, a large sprawling structure.

"Ralph Anders," explained Stream. "Single,

never married. Likes living alone."

"Pretty quiet."

"Here they come. Stand still."

The wolves came drifting from somewhere to stand around Stream and Lou, ignoring him, watching her.

"We're in their territory," she told Lou. Then she sighed.

"Time to remove something from existence."

Stream stepped from the forest and strode quickly across the clearing and up onto the front porch.

The wolf pack ambled along with her, ears up and twitching around, listening for sounds.

Lou hurried after them and up to her side. He had been watching what was happening so intently he forgot to follow.

A few of the wolves sniffed at his pants as he passed them, but that was all they did.

Stream reached out and tried the front door knob. It turned easy. She opened the door slowly.

Lou yanked out his gun.

"I don't think that you will need that," she said as she opened the door as wide as it would go.

The wolf pack flowed into the house.

Stream held out an arm to keep Lou from following them.

"No! You stay with me."

From deep inside the house they heard a scream, then nothing.

Stream stepped into the house consulting a piece of paper.

"This way." She led him to the kitchen and pointed at the outside door. "Stand over there, Lou."

She turned on one of the burners on the stove and watched it light. Then she turned it off, reached into a pocket and handed Lou a candle and a box of matches.

"By the wall, just inside the front door. Set the lighted candle on the floor, anchor it there with some of the melted wax. Then close that door firmly, but don't blow it out, and come back here. Hurry."

Lou did, and returned shortly.

"Open the outside door."

He did. And jerked.

Wolves came from somewhere in the house and trotted out into the grass.

Stream waited, then satisfied that the entire pack was out there, she turned on a burner on the stove and blew out the blue flame.

Propane hissed into the kitchen.

"Outside!"

She dashed out the door and slammed it shut behind him.

"Now we run!"

She charged back up the jeep-trail they had walked in, wolves trotting along with her. Lou jogged at the back of the pack.

In short order, it seemed to him, they ran into the

intersection, turned and headed down the road, stilling running.

After they had gone some distance, Stream slowed up and began to walk, breathing deeply.

As she walked she yanked out a map, took a quick check, and pointed. "Should be a branch right around this jog in the road."

There was.

Stream hurried down the branch road.

Lou hurried after her.

They were surrounded by the pack.

"This one," she explained, "is James Laparona. His wife died not too long ago. Two daughters, grown up with careers on the east coast. He should be alone."

As they approached the opening, Lou could see that this house was of a more modest size than the other one. To one side of the house they could see a large garden with high deer fencing all around.

Right in the middle of the garden a man was working. The wide gate was thrown open. A large garden cart was parked next to it.

The wolf pack poured into the garden area and stopped, all eyes focused on the man who had jerked to his feet, eyes flying wide. He turned and watched as Stream and Lou approached.

Before he could speak, Stream asked, "James L., I presume?"

"All these dogs belong to you or to him?"

Stream stopped in the gate opening.

"I wish to speak to James L."

"Inside the house."

She waved at Lou.

He ran toward and inside the house.

"I wouldn't move, if I was you," she cautioned.

He nodded at her and stood perfectly still.

In a few moments Lou came out and called, "Nobody home."

The man shrugged.

"O.K.," he said. "Talk to me."

"You James?"

"I am. And you are?"

"Stream."

He stared at her. "You?"

"Yep."

"What are you doing here? With this large pack of mutts?"

Lou stepped to her side, gun in hand.

"Shall I shoot him?" he asked.

"No need."

James L. was reaching inside his jacket when he disappeared under a tangle of wolves.

Stream turned away and headed back up the jeep-trail, beginning to run.

"One to go."

Lou jogged after her.

"You all right?" she asked him as he jogged up to run along her side.

"Yep. But I don't understand how you do that.

What you are doing with those wolves and all."

"I'll tell you after we are done with his neighbor and we are back inside the wilderness headed for home."

She waggled one hand.

"Lou, there will be no bodies. It will just be one of those fascinating mysteries. Three men living rather isolated up in the woods who disappeared.

In the distance they heard a soft thump. Stopping, turning, they could see a column of smoke beginning to rise.

"We better hurry," said Stream. "The fire fighters from the forest service will get here pretty soon."

They did. Hurry. Racing down the jeep trail.

As they approached their final destination, Stream halted, said something, and the wolf pack stopped.

She led Lou into the clearing.

They faced a two story structure done in Swiss chalet style.

A tell man dressed in a grey business suit stood on a second story balcony peering at the plume of smoke through large binoculars.

Stream started for the house.

"Lou, you stay outside and keep the front door open. I am going inside to talk with Ztrich. Divorced. One grown son who is into computers and works in Silicon Valley in California, rarely, if ever, visits."

She opened the door and hurried inside, down

the hall, and up the stairs.

Lou looked around and took one of the large boulders that apparently were being used as decorative elements on the porch and set it against the wide open door. Then he added another one just because he felt like it. That door wasn't going anywhere. Now. No need to babysit it.

Holding his gun down along his right side, he walked out onto the lawn to where he could watch the balcony and had a good sight line on the man up there. He saw her step out.

"Hi there, Ztrich," she said. "I came for a short visit."

He turned to face her and carefully set the binoculars on the deck of the balcony.

He nodded. And took a sip from his coffee cup, fetched from the balcony railing.

"That plume of smoke your doing?"

"Yep."

He nodded. "Then I assume that you must be the Stream we have been hearing about." He waggled a free hand at her. "Well, more or less. We never got a good picture of you, but who else would be way up here, visiting, and, ah, causing a problem."

She smiled at him.

"Well, Ztrich, as the saying goes, turn about is fair play."

He nodded and took a sip. Then he turned the cup around in his hands.

"I have had this coffee cup," he said, smiling a very sad smile, "for a very long time. I'd like you to take it with you when you leave." He nodded. "I assume from your last statement that I am about to die."

"Yep."

He bent and set the coffee cup next to the binoculars. As he straightened up, he reached inside his jacket, and yanked out a gun.

His head exploded upward.

Lou had fired from below where he had been watching Ztrich very carefully and maintaining a good sight line at the same time.

The body tumbled to the deck of the balcony.

Stream bend over and heaved the limp body up and over the railing.

She shrugged, bend over, and took the coffee cup, and stuffed it into a large side pocket.

Then she leaned on the railing and called down to Lou, "Find a bucket, fill it with water and bleach, and bring it up here, please."

After they cleaned the balcony and dumped the water into one of the flower beds, they ran back up the road.

Stream stopped and ran back to the wolf pack, now circling around the body on the grass, and talked to them.

Spinning away, she hurried up to Lou.

"Let's go camping, partner. Then I will tell you all about what Special Child really means, just like I promised."

Days later, she was driving along a dirt road, one of the poorly maintained dirt roads in this rather empty, in terms of roads, piece of New Mexico.

She was driving rather slowly, knowing that there would be no traffic piling up behind her, and that it would easier on her truck if she didn't batter it to death by driving too fast.

The CD in her radio system was playing through its speakers, one of Nakai's flute albums. It seemed to her to be appropriate. She looked over and winked at Lou.

As she rattled along and across the ruts and bumps, she noticed, now and then, the tire tracks leaving the road and headed out into a open space to somewhere unseen from the road.

At the correct spot she would do the same thing.

They were taking time off, a vacation, some more time off, some more vacation.

Finally she was there, the correct spot. She turned off the road onto the rarely used parallel ruts that were tire tracks.

She arrived, parked in the usual place, the one she always used when coming here. Other than the twin ruts nothing was visible from that dirt road.

She unloaded her gear, set it on the ground next to her rig, inhaled a deep breath of the clear desert air, and began to organize whatever required organizing.

Lou did the same thing.

After locking the truck, shrugged on her pack, and set out, walking in the faint game trail that headed exactly toward where she was going. She inhaled deeply, tasting the odors of the sparse vegetation drifting past her, hissed it out, turned her head as she walked and listened to the various small birds darting about, making their small bird calls, from clump to clump of brush.

Lou followed her.

For her, this was an easy hike, one she had made a number of times before. She strode along with a easy hiker's stride, slowly, slowly, sinking below the surrounding surface until she stood on the bottom of a very narrow, high-walled canyon, or draw, or crack, however one might wish to label it. The colors blended from soft rust brown to slight tans where water had washed down from above dragging along other colors.

Lou stepped to her side and carefully checked their surroundings.

She had checked and rechecked the weather forecasts for this area, using a number of different sources. No rain was forecast stretching well past the time they would spend here. There were numbers of cracks and crevices that would allow water to pour down into this canyon. Not something to look forward to if one was down here.

It would take them several hours before they got there.

So, she strolled along, talking with him, watching

the play of light on the high walls, listening to various sounds, coming from here and there, and relaxed, really, really relaxed.

Which, after all, was the reason for being here.

It was about two hours of casual strolling before they arrived.

She stopped and carefully checked the immediate area, and satisfied that no-one had been, or was , around, she strolled further down the canyon and turned to face one the vertical canyon walls where water seeped from the thin crack and into a carved stone bowl. Refilling her water bottle, then his, she turned and walked back and around the sharp bend in the canyon.

Standing in front of the pock-marked stone face she carefully explained how and where he had to place his hands and feet. She watched and gave him corrections as he made his way upward. And waited until he slipped over the edge and disappeared inside. Then she began to climb, carefully placing her hands and feet into the correct spots among the many indentations.

It was a very careful ascent, one that she had worked out over many days of frustration after she had the realization what it was that she saw. That realization had come from her intensive reading in the archaeological literature of this area, and a recognition, one that she had gained from much trail and error, and hard work, of the correct path up to her, and the ancient dwellers of this place, living spot, her camping spot.

At the top of her climb, she slithered over the lip of the great cavern and stood and smiled at him. "Good job. It is a difficult climb."

She walked around checking for footprints in the back area, protected from the weather outside. The only footprints were those she had left from past trips. Back here there was always a faint dust dry smell.

Satisfied that these abandoned dwellings had not been disturbed, she set her pack against a house wall and made camp and spread out her sleeping gear. Lou did the same thing.

She pointed across the open space to the far wall at the great panel of petroglyphs made in the far distant past by those who had lived here. Strange figures, designs, and animals, the meanings of which were unknown but written about by researchers throughout the United States who often "explained" them mainly utilizing their imaginations.

"There they are."

Lou nodded and walked over to take a closer look and to inspect them.

Stream thought that this was a good spot to camp, so she explained it to Lou.

Even if the weather, in spite of the several forecasts, should suddenly shift and the canyon ran wet, she would be dry. This cavern was high above the high water marks. If the wind blew down or over the high canyon walls, the depth of the cavern and the structure it held tended to buffer such storms and kept the rear area dry. And if she had to, she could follow the route that original dwellers had used to get to the upper surface, where wet would not be such a hazard to the health. It would be another very careful climb.

She sat and leaned back again the wall.

"Well, partner, here you are, just like I told you."

"Interesting place." He walked back from his inspection and sat next to her.

They made and ate dinner, then sat side by side on the lip of the cavern, legs dangling down, and watched darkness begin to flood the canyon. Looking up, they could see the brightest stars beginning to show in the ever darkening sky.

She hitched back, stood, walked over and arranged her sleeping gear into the correct shape, stretched out, and just before she fell asleep, she laughed.

"What?" Lou rolled up onto his side and looked at her.

"Maybe the Katchinas will visit you."

About the Author

George R. Mead began to study anthropology in 1962 after being discharged (honorably) from the U. S. Army, Combat Engineers. He eventually received a B.A., M. A., and Ph. D. in his chosen field, before that an A.A. in Engineering. And many years later an M. S. W. in Clinical Social Work. He has worked in aerospace, taught at the college and university levels, worked in a community action agency, ran a restaurant, been unemployed, and worked for the U. S. Forest Service. He is now retired from the work-a-day world but does a certain amount of consulting, writing, and research. He lives seven miles outside of the small town of La Grande, Oregon, with his wife, two cats, and one dog from the animal shelter, Kona.